RANCHER TAKES HIS LAST CHANCE AT LOVE

THE RANGERS OF PURPLE HEART RANCH BOOK 6

SHANAE JOHNSON

THOSE JOHNSON GIRLS

Edited by Alyssa Breck

Manufactured in the United States of America
First Edition November 2020

*R*usty Hook turned his cell phone over and over in his palm. His palms were sweaty, and there was a tremor in the ring finger of his left hand as the plastic case of the phone scraped against the gold band on his hand. His wedding band lifted a fraction each time the phone case bumped against it, but the ring kept its spot low on his finger, where it had been for the last five years.

"In a situation like this, we'd follow the first three principles of hostage negotiation."

A woman in fatigues stood at the front of the classroom. Her blunt fingertips pointed at the colorful slides of a Powerpoint presentation as she went through her points. Her gaze flicked over at Rusty as she spoke.

"Those principles are to contain, isolate, and negotiate," the soldier went on. "The method was successfully executed during an operation in Afghanistan where Sergeant Hook negotiated the safe return of four young boys stolen to become child soldiers."

Rusty didn't raise his head to acknowledge his part in the training presentation. Though this was his class on crisis management tactics while in the theater of combat, his eyes were on the wedding band contained on his finger. It sat isolated in that spot. There was no room to negotiate its release from his hand, even if the woman who put it there had asked him to take it off.

"You could argue that Sergeant Hook tacked on the principle of surrender when he demanded the release of the children in his negotiations."

If only that tactic worked with the female species. For months, Rusty had tried every negotiation tactic he'd ever employed to win back one hostage. But he couldn't seem to contain her, as she refused to stay in one place. He had no opportunity to isolate her, as they were always on opposite ends of the country, or sometimes the world. She wouldn't talk to him to negotiate any terms of surrender.

Until a few days ago.

His phone vibrated in his hands. He'd turned the ringer off while he sat in the presentation. He didn't accept the call. One look at the caller ID button told him that that particular call could wait. He had to keep the line open for the call he truly wanted.

"Negotiations account for ninety-seven percent of safe release cases. When those tactics don't work, the escalation tactics of using chemicals to flush out the enemy, or sharpshooters to wound or kill, have a far less success rate."

A few days ago, Rusty had gotten a call. It was an unexpected call as he'd been trying to flush out this particular adversary for months. When he'd seen her name on the caller ID, it had been like a round straight to the heart. He'd answered before the first ring was complete and set to giving her anything she wanted.

"If you can get the combatant to talk, the best place for you to be is not with them, but up high and out of sight."

Rusty scoffed at that. Being apart from his estranged wife was the last thing he wanted. Getting her onto his territory was his number one goal. She was coming here, driving from wherever she had been hiding out from him.

Just the thought of her driving that death trap she refused to give up gave Rusty a case of the jitters. He was sure she hadn't changed the oil since the last time he'd done it for her. She didn't know how to put more air in a tire, much less think about rotating them. What if she broke down on one of these long Montana backroads with no service station for miles?

"And lastly, as Sergeant Hook has taught us time and again, you have to be willing to walk away from any negotiation."

Rusty's head jerked up at that. Had he uttered those words? He had no intention of ever walking away from Ronnie. No matter how far she ran from him. But she wasn't running anymore. She was coming back to him.

Not to get back with him. The divorce papers she'd sent months ago had made her stance on their marriage clear. But she needed him for something. Whatever it was, he was going to give it to her. He wouldn't be able to help himself. Married or separated, his every instinct still was to give her the world.

With the presentation over, Rusty ducked outside before any of the workshop participants could corner him. The sun was reaching its peak on this fall day in Montana. Behind him, he could hear the grunts of men and women as they were put through their paces on the obstacle course of the Boots on the Ground Training Camp that prepared soldiers to undergo the arduous rigors of the Army Ranger School.

For a long time, Rusty had felt that the time he spent in the mud and climbing over barriers had been the hardest thing he'd ever done. Harder even than his many tours and missions in war-ravaged foreign lands. He'd been wrong. The hardest moment of his life was waiting for his phone to ring.

"Why didn't you pick up my call?"

Rusty looked up at the man coming toward him. Anthony Keaton's blue eyes were locked on the phone in Rusty's hands.

"Oh," said Keaton. "I see."

Rusty let out a long sigh as he flipped the phone once more in his palm. He'd turned the ringer back on. But the phone remained silent.

"That's happening today?" asked Keaton.

Rusty gave a nod, not trusting his voice. Which was funny. He was a trained hostage negotiator. More than half of his skills were in talking. This had been one problem he'd never been able to work out. Likely because he was the hostage in this situation.

He felt powerless. The uncertainty of his future plagued him. He'd never been on this side of the table in a crisis situation.

"Why don't you take the day off?" said Keaton. "We've got this."

"No," said Rusty. "I need something to occupy my mind while..."

He held up his phone as though it would finish the sentence for him. It still remained silent, allowing the ellipsis of Rusty's sentence to drag on. Keaton clapped him on the back, three times as though to put an emphasis on that punctuation.

"She didn't say what this was about?" asked Keaton.

Rusty shook his head. He noted that Keaton didn't use his wife's name. There had been a time while they'd served together that every other word out of Rusty's mouth had been about Veronica. As his tours got longer and more frequent, he'd spoken her name aloud less and less. That never changed the fact that she was still in his every waking thought, his sleeping ones as well.

"You don't think she's changed her mind?" Keaton's words were measured and slow. His expression told Rusty that he was trying to sound nonchalant, but Rusty caught the barely masked note of hope in his friend's voice.

Keaton liked Ronnie. All the guys in his unit liked his wife. Everyone who met her liked her. Rusty just wasn't sure why his wife had stopped liking him.

He wished Ronnie had changed her mind. It had taken him months to finally see the writing on the wall. It all became clear to him when he'd received the divorce paperwork with her signature on the line.

It was more than the fact that she'd signed the paperwork. It was how she'd signed it. Where Ronnie had always placed a heart over the I in her name, it was now just a solid, black dot.

"Well, we're all good here at camp," said Keaton. "But Dylan and Dr. Patel had been asking for you to help with a matter up on the Purple Heart Ranch."

That was as good a place to be as any. Rusty remembered his first day here on the Purple Heart Ranch; the rehabilitation ranch for wounded veterans. His team of six had been lucky in that they'd walked onto the ranch without any physical injuries. Though they all had scars. Rusty's injury was internal. He'd come with a broken heart.

The funny thing was that this ranch was

renowned for more than only healing injuries of the wounded. The soldiers who stayed often found their true love while rehabilitating their bodies.

Rusty knew the ranch's matchmaking magic would never work on him. He'd found the love of his life years ago. His problem was that he lost her and he didn't know why?

He mounted one of the horses they kept to move from the training camp to the ranch. He tucked his phone in his pocket and gave a tug of the reins to get the animal moving. But as the horse took off, the communication device slipped from Rusty's pocket. The clomping of the horse's hooves as they galloped away muted the ringing of his phone.

CHAPTER TWO

*R*onnie Hook pursed her lips at the sound of the phone ringing in her ear. By the fourth ring, she was gritting her teeth. When the beep that indicated the answering service had engaged, she blew out a disappointed breath.

There was silence after the beep. Rusty never bothered to record a voice message, not even when they'd dated. He wasn't the share-your-feelings type. He certainly wasn't a leave-a-recording-of-your-thoughts type.

If he needed to leave a message, he'd hold it in his head until he saw her. When they'd married, he'd barely made it through the home phone message she'd insisted on recording. He'd even frowned at the mounted device hanging on the kitchen wall, certain no one of importance would ever call. He'd sounded stilted as they recorded the outgoing message.

Hi, this is Veronica...and Russell.

Sorry, you missed us... but stay on the line.

To cast a message for...the Hooks.

They'd gotten a lot of chuckling compliments for that message. Well, only about five since hardly anyone ever used the landline's number. But that voice message had been the encapsulation of their relationship. Ronnie was the bubbly romantic, while Rusty was always measured and practical.

It had been that calm, quiet attitude that had drawn her to him when they'd first met. Ronnie's life had always been a deafening hurricane with the large family she'd come from. She'd been born smack dab in the middle of seven siblings. Her oldest sister and youngest brother got all of the attention, while Ronnie was often forgotten. Mainly because she always had her nose in a book, and often chose obscure places to read, like the linen closet, or under the kitchen cabinets, or the crawlspace in the attic. But those places were where she could find quiet and solitude in the madhouse that was her home.

When she'd gone off to live with Rusty, all had been blessedly quiet. There had also been a good deal of solitude. It took years before the lonely silence became a problem—years before she felt his long absences acutely. By then, it was too late.

Ronnie would not be dealing with his silence any longer. She hit redial on her cellphone. The phone intoned the numbers Ronnie knew by heart. Rusty hadn't changed his phone number since they were dating. Even though he preferred text messages, he'd always answered on the first ring.

Once again, the phone rang and rang in Ronnie's ear. Four rings, a beep, and a standard voice message from the female computerized voice telling her to leave a message at the tone. Ronnie pressed End and pushed her phone away from her.

"Can I get you anything else, hon?"

Ronnie looked up at the waitress. She was a middle-aged woman with gray at the roots of her hair. Her smile was matronly, but her figure was anything but. The waitress, Marla as told by her name tag, had the slender form and height that Ronnie had always wished for but never rose to.

Ronnie only barely crested five feet, and a lot of that was achieved by the riot of brown curls atop her head. She had a slim waist, but above her belly was cleavage one cup size away from making her top-heavy. To balance that out, her hips were what was kindly referred to as good for childbearing.

Ronnie was an hourglass where she'd always wanted to be a vase. Vases held roses. All hourglasses ever held was sand.

But Ronnie didn't hold her figure against Marla. The waitress had given Ronnie extra guacamole on her burrito, so Ronnie was leaving her a big tip.

"No, I'm done," Ronnie said. "I'll take the check."

Marla tore a slip and placed it on the table. But when she went to pull away, one of the bangles on her wrist caught Ronnie's satchel. The avocado in Ronnie's stomach turned as she watched her bag fall the short distance to the hard floor.

Marla reached for the bag and caught the straps. Relief flooded the older woman's face. Ronnie's features pulled tighter together in absolute horror.

Though Marla had saved the bag from its date on the pristine floor, the contents of the bag spilled out. There was only one thing inside of Ronnie's bag. Ronnie shuddered when it impacted the unforgiving ground.

There wasn't the shattering crack of glass breaking. Nor was there the metallic clang of precious jewelry hitting the floor. There was simply a thud, the sound of the hard spine of a book fracturing as its pages were ruffled.

As though the book was aware it had been caught naked out in public, the covers squeezed its pages back in. For a second, Ronnie thought the book would stand upright, but it teetered on the edge of its spine. Ronnie held her breath, hoping against hope that it would land on its face, thus hiding the cover.

But no. The book fell on its back. Hiding the blurb of the story inside the pages. Most people judged the book by its cover, anyway.

Marla's perfectly plucked brows rose to her gray hairline as she looked down at the vivid jewel tones of the cover. When Ronnie had printed it at an Office Depot Store, she was surprised at how bright the colors turned out. So bright that the couple depicted in the image looked orange.

"Is that one of those alien romance novels?" asked the man in the booth across from her. "I heard about those." He gave her a wink before dipping his tortilla chip into a bowl of salsa.

Ronnie sat frozen in her seat. She vacillated between the shame at Marla's pinched gaze and outrage at the man's lascivious stare. The dueling emotions didn't allow her to move to pick up the book.

"I'll just cover that up for you." Marla reached for a napkin, then the book.

As the waitress held the book gingerly, the pages fluttered again. Inside, Ronnie saw a copious amount of red markings, notes for mistakes on the manuscript. So much red that the book looked as though it was bleeding. Marla slid the injured tome back into Ronnie's satchel, as though it were a bandage, and placed it on the table.

Ronnie didn't meet the woman's eyes as Marla collected her dirty dishes. Ronnie was used to the judgment over her reading material. As a kid, she had had many a book yanked from her hands by her parents, her siblings, teachers, and librarians.

You're not old enough for that, said her mother.

That's mine, said her older sister.

That's above your reading level, said the librarians.

That's not on the assignment we're working on, said her teachers.

But with the invention of the ebook, no one could see what she was reading. Ronnie had downloaded hundreds of romance books and devoured every single one of them. So much to the point that she thought she could write one herself.

And so she had.

Using a pen name, of course. She might love the romance genre, but she didn't need any more grief from her family and friends about her reading habit, or now her new career. Her book just needed a professional cover, one not created by her in Microsoft Word. It also needed a qualified editor, which would cost money she didn't have...yet.

She looked down at her phone. It wasn't like Rusty to not answer her calls. Definitely not like him to not call her back.

But she had no claim to him any longer. They'd been separated for nearly a year. They were getting a divorce. She'd signed the papers months ago, but Rusty had been dragging his feet.

That had frustrated Ronnie, until now. She needed him to cosign a business loan so that she could get the money to make her dreams come true. After that, he would have to let her get on with her life. And he would get on with his.

Ronnie was here to get two signatures from him. The first on a loan. The second on the divorce papers.

She hadn't wanted to do this face to face. Rusty had a habit of talking her into what he wanted. That was his job as a hostage negotiator. But she'd held still and quiet in this relationship too long waiting for him to come home to her. Meanwhile, he went all around the world solving crisis after crisis, while back at home, she stewed alone in the silence.

Love shouldn't be quiet. Ronnie didn't want to go back to the quiet, and there was nothing Rusty could say to make her turn around. Now, she had something to say, and she'd written it all down in a book. A book with a bright cover and bleeding words that she wanted to share with the world...after muting the color a bit and cleaning up the manuscript.

Ronnie knew where Rusty was staying; a place called the Purple Heart Ranch. It was just a half-hour drive away. She grabbed her purse and her book and headed out to her car.

Climbing inside her old Chevy named Old Bessie, the engine wheezed as Ronnie turned the key. After a few false starts, the engine roared to life. And by roar, it let out a grumble that made a few pedestrians jump back.

The check engine light came on as Ronnie

pulled out onto Main Street. But Bessie was reliable. The old girl would get her to her destination. Once Ronnie had her first royalty check from her published book, she'd get her car a complete internal makeover.

CHAPTER THREE

The ride across the green pasture did much to settle Rusty's mind. There was something about being up on a horse that sent power up through the legs. Many of the riders he encountered on the way to the Purple Heart Ranch had lost limbs. But astride the therapy horses, it was clear to see that their wounds hadn't broken their spirits.

It wasn't just the horses that helped these men and women take back the power of their lives. Soldiers and veterans worked in a garden, digging gnarled and mangled fingers into rich soil and pulling up vegetables they produced through hard work. Men and women with scars and burn marks tended to livestock that cared not for their looks but for the care and attention given.

This place was a paradise for service members and their families. It was a place that Ronnie would've loved to live in. Maybe if he brought her here, she might fall in love with the ranch and back in love with him?

Rusty brought the horse down to a slow trot as he approached the stables. Before Rusty could dismount, he got waved down by Dylan Banks and Dr. Patel. Rusty climbed down from the horse and handed him over to one of the ranch hands. Then he approached the two men.

Dylan Banks stood in a pair of cargo shorts. The cool fall breeze wisped through the gears of his prosthetic leg. Dark circles formed a half-moon under his eyes, but the man looked too joyful to be tired. Rusty knew Dylan awaited the birth of his second child. The smile on his face was that of a man who had everything in life he ever wanted. Once upon a time, Rusty had known that smile for himself.

After shaking hands with Dylan, Rusty turned to the smaller man beside him. Dr. Patel wore a serene smile as ever. The man also wore a tweed jacket, making him look more like a college professor than a psychologist. What did look out of place was the hint of concern in his gaze.

"We're glad you're here," said Dylan. "We could use a man with your skills."

"Is there a problem?" Rusty's particular skillset was only ever called upon in times of trouble. It often involved a ransom note, suicide vest, or hostages. None of that was in alignment with this healing ranch.

"We just had a new patient come into the clinic," said Patel. "He's come off a rough mission and has a past documented TBI."

TBIs, or traumatic brain injury, were the bane of a soldier's existence. Just as in sports, there were often collisions of linebackers and forwards, bombs exploding, and hand-to-hand combat were murder on the brain. The problem in the military was that for a long time, these sneaky wounds went undetected and silently degraded the health of many a serviceman.

"He was starting to improve," said Dylan, his expression going grave. "But then he got word that his wife had signed divorce papers."

Rusty remembered that particular gut punch when he'd received those documents in the mail from the woman he'd sworn to love and protect his whole life. He'd never been diagnosed with a TBI, but that moment he'd felt as though the pieces of paper were shrapnel burning his fingers.

"We thought with your area of expertise, along with your recent experience with... you know." Dylan looked away instead of saying the D-word.

"I understand," Rusty chimed in, not meeting either man's eyes. "Just say the word, and I'm happy to have a chat with him."

Rusty tried to inject cheer into his voice. That failed. Because he'd failed. His number one job had been to make his wife happy, and he'd failed.

He caught Dylan's eye then. Dylan had found the love of his life here on this ranch. So had many of the soldiers who lived here. Each marriage was strong and happy. Back at the Vance Ranch, the same thing had happened. Each of his friends had fallen madly, hopelessly in love, and gotten married only days after meeting the woman they hadn't dared to dream of.

Maybe that could happen to Rusty. But he'd have to clear Veronica out of his heart. And there simply wasn't a broom large enough for the task. She was in every nook and cranny of his chest.

Dylan gave Rusty a clap on the back. Then he

turned and took off. Likely in search of his wife and child.

Dr. Patel, however, stayed behind and eyed Rusty closely.

Rusty and his team had never been through the Purple Heart Ranch's healing program. They hadn't come here wounded physically. His team had come with the express purpose to train soldiers at their camp. But they'd gotten close to the residents, including the resident psychologist who liked to meddle in not only everyone's mental state but in their affairs of the heart as well.

"How are you doing these days?" said Patel.

Rusty wasn't used to being the one to answer questions. He was the one who did the talking and listening in a hostage negotiation.

"I hear you signed the divorce papers?"

Rusty nodded. "I did. A few days ago."

"I also hear your wife is coming for a visit."

There were no secrets in this place. You told a wall a private matter, it would carry over to the next roof by the end of the day, and every human, child, and animal would know your business.

"She says she needs a favor," said Rusty. "I'll always do anything for her, regardless of whether we're legally married or not."

"Just because you sign a document, that doesn't mean the heart stops wanting what it wants."

Wasn't that the truth? Rusty knew he would never love another woman again in this lifetime. Even though he'd signed the papers, he still considered Veronica his wife.

'Til death, he'd pledged.

'Til death, he meant.

"If you need anything, I'm here for you," said Patel. And with that, the older man turned on his heel and headed toward the ranch's clinic.

Rusty watched him go. He had to admit he was a little surprised. He'd expected more probing and prodding from the psychologist. But that was it.

Maybe there was no hope for Rusty's situation? He patted his pocket for his phone. It had been thirty minutes since he'd last checked for it. His hand ran over the smooth fabric. There was no rectangular indentation in his jeans.

His phone wasn't there. His sole connection to Ronnie was gone. What if she'd called and he'd missed it? Panic set in.

Rusty turned to retrace his steps. He had ridden the horse for a long distance here. It could be anywhere.

He looked up and got distracted by what he saw.

A man was on the roof of the barn. The man walked dangerously close to the edge. Rusty didn't think, he acted.

He raced inside the structure, climbing up until he was at the roof. He stepped out onto the roof and called out to the man.

What had Dylan said his name was?

"Randy?" The man didn't answer to that.

"Ray?" Still no response.

"Reggie." That was it. But still, the man didn't answer.

That was a bad sign. When the party didn't speak, it meant they'd already given up hope. Much like how Ronnie had stopped speaking to Rusty. She'd given up hope on their marriage a year ago and simply stopped responding to his pleas for another chance.

Reggie took another step and looked over the side. The roof was high enough that a break of some body part was likely. But he didn't step over. He only peered down. Maybe the man just wanted attention?

Suddenly Reggie turned to look over his shoulder. He peered at Rusty as if he was just noticing him for the first time, even though Rusty had been calling out to him.

"Listen, Reggie, let's talk about this."

Reggie reached up to his ears. He pinched his fingers into first the left and then the right ear, pulling wireless earbuds out. "What are you doing up here?"

"I'm here to help, Reggie," said Rusty.

"My name is Paul. I'm here to fix the roof. Who are you?"

Rusty was just a few feet from the man. He'd had his hands outstretched, trying to portray a non-threatening posture. But he let that go under this revelation.

"You're a roofer?"

Paul nodded.

"Not a soldier?"

Paul shook his head.

Rusty let out a sigh. He felt like a complete idiot. Here he was trying to save someone who was just doing their job. And it appeared they'd obtained an audience. There was a small crowd gathering down below. In the crowd, he saw a familiar head of curly brown hair.

Ronnie?

He didn't think. He took a step toward her. And fell off the roof.

CHAPTER FOUR

*W*hen Ronnie pulled up to the Purple Heart ranch, she assumed it would be like any base she'd ever lived on. She'd lived on a lot of bases. Such was the life of a military wife.

But the houses she drove by looked modern and not like something from three decades ago. In a lot of the military housing she'd experienced, the appliances were older than her parents, and the laundry room had to be entered into with a gas mask due to the rank smell of unclean socks and underwear come back from overseas.

Here on this base, that wasn't a base at all but a ranch, couples strolled by, sneaking kisses. Children played ball with a group of dogs running between their legs. A gathering of women sat off to the side, sipping drinks out of decorative mugs. Smiles warmed their faces.

As Ronnie drove by, one of the women looked up and waved. Ronnie ducked her head and focused on fitting her oversized Chevy into the parking space.

Military bases were always a tight-knit community. The wives there were often the stitching holding the fabric together. Ronnie missed having that group of friends most. She was still in touch with the wives she'd befriended over the years. But email and phone calls just didn't do it. And that's why she had no intention of moseying up to those women to collect more people who would eventually be pulled away from her in the line of duty.

"Hi!"

Ronnie looked up to see the woman who'd waved to her, standing at her driver's side window. There was a small bump beneath her shirt that could only be from pregnancy.

"Can I help you find where you're going?"

The woman's voice was pleasant. Not that Ronnie would've expected anything different from a military wife. Even though this wasn't a base, its people still had all the hallmarks.

The women at the table leaned back, eying the

two of them. Ronnie didn't second guess their welcoming smiles. She just didn't want to get attached to something temporary. She would only be here for a couple of days at most.

"I'm looking for someone," said Ronnie.

"What's their name?"

"Russell Hook."

The woman's face split into a beatific grin. "Oh, you're Rusty's wife?"

"No. Yes. Not anymore. Can you tell me where he lives?"

Her smile didn't dim at Ronnie's denial. "He doesn't live on this ranch. He lives next door on the Vance Ranch. But he works here. It's just a hike to get to the training camp. Let me find someone to drive you over there."

Ronnie followed the woman, Maggie she learned her name was. She also learned that Maggie had a son and a daughter on the way. She learned that Maggie had lived on the ranch for a couple of years now.

Ronnie let Maggie go on as she tried to keep at least a foot of distance between herself and the friendly woman. The friendship that beckoned between them would not survive after Ronnie completed her business here. And that business would conclude as soon as she got Rusty's signature, once she found him.

And then she saw him.

Rusty stood on top of a roof. He had his hands outstretched. It was a posture she knew well. It was the same posture he'd used when she'd told him she wanted a divorce. He'd tried to talk her down. He'd tried to use his hostage negotiation tactics on her.

He'd used her name over and over again. He'd tried to get her talking, to keep an open line of communication between them. But by then, there had been nothing more to say. She couldn't bear to watch him leave another time. So that time, she'd left.

It didn't look like his tactics were working now. The man near the ledge appeared to be ignoring Rusty's attempts to save his life. The man was standing very close to the edge.

"Should we call someone," said Ronnie.

"That's the roofer," said Maggie. "What's Rusty doing up there?"

The roofer finally turned to acknowledge Rusty. Ronnie couldn't hear what the exchange between the two was. She was far too focused on her soon to be ex-husband.

He'd lost weight. But even with the loss of the

pounds, his shoulders were still as broad as a bear's. She knew exactly where the warmest spot in his chest was where she could hibernate all winter.

Except they never got to hibernate all winter. He was always called away. She was always left alone, moving, setting up a new life, new friends where she would wait for him to come back so they could repeat the whole process again.

Not anymore. She'd turned away from that life. No, she wasn't exactly happier. Yet. But she would be. Soon.

Ronnie was about to turn away from Rusty on the roof when their gazes connected. Ronnie's heart did that flip every time she was in his presence. The flip hadn't gone away even when things had gone silent between them. Her mind might be made up, but her heart had never gotten with the program. Even though it broke every time he got spun up and walked away from her to go on a mission.

Her heart flipped again when Rusty took a step toward her. It flipped because Rusty didn't seem to remember that he was on a slanted roof and not solid ground. With a second step toward her, his feet came out from under him, and he fell.

Rusty landed with a sickening thud to the ground. Ronnie ran toward him, her heart in her throat. When she got to him, he lay immobile on the ground.

There was a crowd around him. Mostly other large males. Likely soldiers. With their big bodies, it was hard to break through them to get to Rusty.

"Make space," said an older man. He was thin with brown skin and a slight accent. The men let the man through, and he reached for Rusty's wrist. "He's breathing. Let's get him to the clinic."

Luckily, her position made it easier to get around the crowd and follow them. Ronnie raced behind them. Rusty's hand dangled between the men who carried him. It was his left hand that dangled. On his ring finger sat his wedding ring. There was a speck of dirt that muted its shine. Ronnie itched to reach over and wipe the spot clean.

"I'm sorry, ma'am. You can't come in."

Ronnie looked up at the imposing soldier. He wasn't one from Rusty's unit. She hadn't seen any of those guys here.

"I'm his wife," she said. It wasn't a lie. They were still married. Rusty hadn't signed the papers. She didn't think he ever would. Now, she was glad of it. But how could she prove that she was who she was?

Ronnie lifted her left hand, only to remember that she'd taken her ring off months ago. It was in her suitcase, inside a hidden compartment with other valuable items. Did she have time to run back to her car and grab it?

"Let her through," said the older man.

The brawny soldier stepped aside, allowing Ronnie to pass. She walked into the room where they laid Rusty out on a bed and stopped just inside the doorway. Rusty lay motionless on the bed, and all Ronnie could do was stand there and stare.

For years, she'd craved silence from her large family so she could escape into a world of books. She'd found that silence with Rusty, and then got restless from his absences. Now here he was, a captive audience, and all she wanted him to do was wake up and shout to make a ruckus.

"Mrs. Hook?"

Ronnie blinked at the elderly man with a stethoscope in his hand. "Yes?"

"I'm Dr. Patel. It doesn't look like anything is broken. But it was a nasty fall. We'll need to wait until he wakes up to be sure."

As though Rusty had heard the older man's command, he started doing just that. His eyes blinked open. His gaze focused on her. His lips split in a wide grin.

"Am I dead?" he asked.

"No, you're alive," said Dr. Patel.

Rusty frowned, his gaze still on Ronnie. "You mean, this isn't heaven?"

"No," chuckled Dr. Patel, "you're on the ranch."

"But she's here, my angel."

Rusty reached his hand up and pulled Ronnie to him. Ronnie didn't resist. Later she'd tell herself that it was because it proved his arms weren't broken. She didn't know what excuse she'd give for why she allowed the man she was trying to divorce to press his lips to hers and kiss her soundly.

CHAPTER FIVE

*H*e was having the dream again.

Each night since Rusty had met his wife six years ago, he'd dreamed of pulling her close and kissing her. Sometimes, in the dream, she would laugh as she kissed him back. Sometimes, as he lay there with his eyes closed, she would sigh and rest her head on his chest.

She did that now in the dream; she sighed as he pressed his lips to hers. Her breath was sweeter than sweet tea. With a hint of avocado. It was Rusty's new favorite treat.

In his dream, he pushed her hair out of her face so that he could get better access to her mouth. There was nothing like Ronnie's big buffet of curls. Her hair was a smorgasbord of spirals. No two coils were alike. The top twisted one way while the back of her frizzed in the opposite direction. Rusty would get lost as he brushed the waves out of her face so that he might claim her lips.

His favorite dream was the one where he tugged back her hair with one hand and handed over a present with the other. The present was a key. The key was to their dream home.

It's what he'd worked for their whole lives together. No more renting a small apartment where they could hear the neighbors every conversation. No more base living where everything was temporary, and as soon as they'd get comfortable, they'd be leaving again (with PCS stickers stuck to more and more of their possessions).

In his dream, Rusty had saved up to buy Ronnie the two-story single-family home of her dreams, complete with a room for a library and a reading nook. Ronnie would look at the house and then turn and kiss him. Just like she was doing now.

Though this dream was far more vivid than the others. He could smell the perfume that she always wore. He felt the silk of her skin as he cupped her cheek. The sweet taste of her had morphed into something spicy; salsa and guacamole.

That was an odd detail that had never come up

in the dream before. And the fingers he ran his hair through felt straighter than normal. But what he did recognize was Veronica's sigh.

Rusty lived for the sound of that sigh of contentment. He hadn't heard it in years. He'd forgotten what it sounded like. But in this dream it all came back to him; the sound of his wife happy and in his arms where she belonged.

A voice cleared somewhere in the distance. How was that? There had never been another person in these dreams. And definitely not a male.

"I beg your pardon." Dr. Patel's voice came from far away, but way too close for this to be in Rusty's imagination. "But, I have to check our patient and make sure everything is intact."

The kiss broke on a gasp. Rusty opened his eyes. And there she was.

Veronica was only a couple of inches away from him. Her wild hair was tamed back into a ponytail. The tendrils were rioting at the edges. But still, she was here. Live and in the flesh... and pulling away from him.

Her eyes blazed brightly. Her cheeks flushed pink. Her lips pursed together, as though they were being scolded for that kiss.

That kiss.

How had that happened? The last thing he remembered was falling from the roof. No, the last thing he remembered was seeing her face in the crowd. Then there had only been the drive to get to her.

Gravity had put a damper on that. Rusty wasn't sure if he was hallucinating or if this was real life. So he let his training kick in, and he asked.

"Are you real?"

"I..." No other words came from her mouth.

Rusty felt the brush of air from her lips. Real or imagined, he knew he was keeping this version of his wife. He would find a way to contain her, to keep her close to him. That was the first step in any hostage negotiation.

"You had a pretty bad fall there, soldier."

Rusty didn't look up at Dr. Patel. He dared not take his eyes off Ronnie. What if she disappeared again.

He had to find a way to move to the next step of hostage negotiation and isolate her. His gaze never left Ronnie as Dr. Patel checked for breaks and sprains in his bones. And then Rusty got his wish. Once he was all checked out, Dr. Patel left the two of them in the room alone.

"Hey," Rusty said.

"Hey," Ronnie said, avoiding his gaze.

"About that kiss—"

"You were dazed," she said, waving his words away.

He was dazed, dazed by her. Ever since the first time he'd seen this woman and her wild hair and huge grin, he had been taken. So taken that he never wanted to be parted from her.

"You don't have to apologize," she said.

Rusty had no intention of apologizing. He'd meant every nibble, every touch of his lips against hers.

"I'm here to talk business. Not about us."

Us? Just as much as he missed kissing his wife, Rusty missed being an us. They weren't an us any longer. Rusty had held out for as long as he could, but he'd eventually given in and signed those divorce papers that separated that monosyllabic word that had tied them together.

"What I need is for you to sign the divorce papers. Since I know you haven't done that yet, I need a favor."

That pulled him up short. Should he tell her that he had signed the papers like she wanted him to? Show her that he was still capable of giving her what she needed. Or should he hold his tongue and see what this favor was? See if there was any leverage he could gain to show her that he was still what she needed?

"I need money," Ronnie said, still not meeting his gaze.

When Ronnie had first called asking for his help, Rusty had wondered for days what she might ask for. He'd assumed she was coming for the divorce papers. Money was the last thing he'd expected to hear. She still had access to all of their banking accounts. He'd never withheld anything from her.

"I told you, whatever alimony-"

"I don't want alimony." Ronnie held up a hand. "I want to take care of myself."

When they'd been dating, Rusty had loved that independent spirit of hers. Ronnie had always insisted on contributing to the family coffers. The problem was she couldn't hold a job. Mainly on account of there always being a book in her hands.

"I want to get a business loan," she continued. "But I'm having problems getting approval since I haven't had steady employment in the past five years as we moved around a lot."

"I don't understand?" Rusty rubbed his palm against his temples. A headache from the fall was starting to grow there. "Why would you take money from strangers at a bank and not out of our account."

"It's not our account. You earned that money."

"You worked for it as well," Rusty insisted. "The life of a military wife is hard work."

"I don't want to argue." Ronnie held up her hand and closed her eyes.

Rusty waited until the pained expression went away. He knew better than to antagonize the person he was trying to negotiate with. He had to find her pain points and show that he was the man to solve them.

"What do you need, Veronica?"

"I just need you to cosign a loan with me."

Easy enough. And the loan document would present another tie to her. He'd take any rope she'd toss his way.

"I know it's an imposition," she said. "It's the last thing I'll ask of you as your wife."

The last thing as his wife? Because she thought she was still his wife. She thought he hadn't signed the papers. But he had. The truth was they were no longer man and wife. But she didn't have to know that yet.

CHAPTER SIX

*R*onnie watched the expressions on Rusty's face. When she'd told him about her intentions to get a business loan, his gaze had narrowed as he searched for understanding in her words. His eyes widened in surprise when she'd declined to use the joint accounts from their marriage, accounts filled with the money he'd earned by risking his life. Didn't he know she couldn't touch that, not when she'd decided to leave him? She'd felt bad enough that she had told him she wanted a divorce before a deployment.

Ronnie had spent those last months in a constant state of despair, expecting to get a knock on the door at any minute. As a military wife, that fear had always been in the back of her mind. But as she'd done for years, she'd soldiered on, just as her husband did during his service. She'd marched forward until she'd hit a brick wall.

Now she sat within reach of her soon to be ex-husband, and she wanted nothing more than to feel his head for bumps from his fall. But that was no longer her right.

Oh, Ronnie knew Rusty would let her. If she had doubted, that kiss they'd shared made his feelings crystal clear. He still wanted her.

Well, she still wanted him. But wanting each other would not solve their problems. So she sat back in her chair.

What do you need, Veronica?

Rusty had always been a rock. No, not a rock. He'd always been like the tree in her parents' backyard. The tree she'd climb early in the morning and sit nestled in its strong branches while she wiled the day away between the pages of a novel.

That was Russell Hook. He was the strongest, sturdiest man she'd ever known. He just couldn't give her what she needed.

Looking at him now, he looked like that same massive tree with thick roots. No matter where they went, it was always Rusty that felt like home. Being in his arms a moment ago had been the first time Ronnie had felt settled in a year.

Ronnie gave herself a shake. This was why she hadn't wanted to see him in person. Things always got confused when she was in his physical presence. They'd never had trouble with the physical aspects of their marriage. It was the emotional aspect where they lacked.

After their first year of marriage, she and Rusty hadn't connected on an emotional level again. After they'd said *I do*, the romance had stopped. They'd settled into a married life of routine. One where he'd split himself in two.

At home, Rusty would kiss her senseless when he was in her presence. On missions, Rusty kept a wall of duty between them that led to a silence that stretched beyond an ocean.

Ronnie knew there had to be a cone of silence surrounding the details of his missions. But that's not what she wanted to get to the heart of. She wanted to get to her husband's heart. Unfortunately, it was buried beneath the layers of his body armor.

"Business loan?" Rusty asked. "What business?"

"I've written a book."

"You have?" His eyes brightened with awe and pride. "That's amazing? I'm so proud of you."

Ronnie's shoulders went back under his praise. There was a part of her that wanted to whip the book out and show it to Rusty, splotchy cover, red marks, and all. But there was another part of her that hesitated. The part of her that hid her romance novel addiction between the covers of a classic tome. The part of her that fist-pumped the air when the eReader was born, and she didn't have to hide so blatantly anymore.

"About what?" Rusty asked. "Life as an army wife?"

"Sort of," Ronnie hedged. Her romance novel did feature a soldier as the hero. The woman he pursued would become his wife by the end of the novel. Which made her character an army wife.

"Oh, I know. It's about the trials of growing up in a large family."

Ronnie cocked her head to the side as though she could see the pages of her book turning. She had grown up in a large family, and that had informed much of her life.

"That's in there, too," she said.

"Tell me more."

But she was tongue-tied.

"Will you let me read it?"

"No." The word was resounding, like slamming a hardback book closed.

"No?" Rusty said, genuine hurt on his face.

"It's not something you'd enjoy reading," she said.

"If you wrote it, I'd enjoy it."

Ronnie bit her lip. "Well, it's not published yet. That's what I need the money for. There are editing costs. And I need to buy cover art. It's all adding up."

"I'll pay for it, whatever the costs."

"No. I want to do this on my own. I can't keep relying on you."

"I'm your husband. It's in the job description."

"You're not my husband anymore." Ronnie turned away from the pain that furrowed his brow. "You won't be soon enough. I can't rely on you anymore."

"You can always rely on me, Veronica. I will always be here for you."

It was words like that that made her heart flip. But Rusty only said things like that when their relationship was in dire straights. The overtures only came out when times were bad. That wasn't the type of romance Ronnie wanted.

"All I want is your signature." She had to force herself to say the next part and inject steel into it.

"Actually, I want your signature twice. First, to cosign the loan. And then, when that's secure, I want you to sign the divorce papers."

Rusty pursed his lips as he regarded her. His gaze was dark. She'd never seen that look on his face.

Ronnie had already used all of the steel in her voice. She didn't have much left for her spine. Rusty was an expert negotiator. He had the skills to talk anyone into or out of anything. He never used those tactics on her. But now he was backed against a wall, being forced to do something he didn't want to. Ronnie was certain he was about to pull out all his hostage negotiating stops.

"All right," he said.

Ronnie blinked. Then cocked her head to peer at him. "All right?"

"It's a deal."

"Deal? Deal as in you mean you'll do it?"

She had expected push back. She had expected him to try to contain her, to isolate her, and then negotiate. She knew the tactics. She knew his tricks. He should've been trying to keep her talking, getting as much information as possible. But he hadn't pried when she'd told him she didn't want him to read the book. He wasn't asking for any details. What was his game?

"We'll go to the bank in the morning," he said. "I'll sign the loan."

"You will?"

"And then in a week, I'll sign the divorce papers."

"A week? Why a week?"

"Because you'll stay here for those seven days and give us a second chance."

There it was. The containment, the isolation, the negotiating leverage he sought. But she knew it was useless.

"It's not going to work, Russ."

Rusty had been the tree that provided her with stability. The roots she knew was her home wherever they were transplanted. The shade that protected her from the elements.

But that was it. Trees weren't inherently romantic. They didn't spout overtures of love. They sprouted leaves. They didn't sweep a girl off their feet. For that, she'd have to climb. And the only place she had to climb was out of this marriage and into a new life of her own.

"Then you have nothing to lose," Rusty said. "You'll have your loan. And in a week, if you haven't changed your mind, we walk away with a clean break and never have to see each other again."

That thought pulled her up short; *never have to*

see each other again. Ronnie wanted the divorce. But the thought of never seeing Russell again hadn't occurred to her. But that is what divorce meant.

"Deal?" he said, holding out his hand.

Ronnie stared at his hand. "Fine."

She put her hand in his. He closed his fingers around hers, and she felt engulfed, safe, secure. And then he let her go, and the feelings went with it.

What had she just gotten herself into?

CHAPTER SEVEN

*R*usty shook out his hand. It was no use. Even all these hours later, he still felt the imprint of Ronnie's hand in his. It was no wonder. The woman was apart of him, had been since the first time he'd pulled her to him and kissed her.

When he'd been deployed for months, that sense of attachment to her had gotten him through many scrapes and long nights.This last year, as he'd felt her slipping away more and more each day, he'd felt himself go hollow in the spots she used to fill.

He'd wanted her back with him. Tucked back into his side. Snuggled back into his chest.

She was back. But she wasn't with him.

Rusty pulled the door to the bunkhouse closed,

leaving Ronnie inside. A part of him wanted to lock the door so that she wouldn't escape. Unfortunately, the lock only worked to keep people out, not in.

Ronnie could leave at any time. And she would. Just as soon as she learned what he'd done.

It was the worst thing that could have happened. Just as Rusty thought he was getting what he wanted, he'd lost the one thing that could change it all. He couldn't find the signed divorce papers.

After months of lugging the thin stack of papers around in his duffle bag, he'd taken them out a few days ago and signed them. The last thing he remembered is stuffing them in an envelope, but he couldn't bring himself to mail them. He'd thought he'd left them on his dresser. When he went into his room, the package wasn't there.

He'd searched the kitchen while Ronnie got settled in Porco's old room. He'd even gone into Spinelli's old room to search. Both Porco and Spinelli were now living with their wives in the cottage on the Verona Commune. Rusty had been the only one in the house for the last couple of days. With each room, he came up empty-handed.

That day when he'd signed the settlement had been such a blur. He couldn't remember much of it. Maybe someone else had come in? By the time he'd finished his search, it had been late. Everyone up at the ranch house would be asleep. Ronnie hadn't left the room after she'd closed the door, indicating there would be no talking between them.

The silent treatment had been her one and only weapon in their marriage. They both knew that if he could get her talking, she'd cave to his requests. Not that Rusty ever made outlandish requests of his wife. All he ever asked her to do when she was upset, or frustrated, or despondent was to stay with him. To wait it out until things got better. Now was that time.

Rusty knew that if he could just talk to his wife, face to face, he could make this better. Ronnie would have to face him today. They had the meeting at the bank later this afternoon. But before the talking, he had to find those papers.

The sun was rising on Vance Ranch as he walked the path from the bungalow to the main house. Ronnie would still be sleeping. She was a night owl, as that was the best time for reading. She wouldn't be up for a few more hours.

Rusty took his time walking the pastures. This morning he couldn't help but take the ranch in with new eyes. Would Ronnie love living someplace like this? There were tons of places for her to curl up and read her books. He'd always dreamed of

53

building her a homestead that was all hers where they could raise their children; curly-haired kids whose noses were always in a book like their mother.

Now, maybe he'd get the chance to make that dream come true. He had seven days to convince her to stay his wife forever. But first, he had to make sure that the paperwork that would dissolve their union could be found and destroyed.

Mac and Lana sat on the porch eating a breakfast of steak and eggs. Mac chewed his meat while gazing at his wife. In his hand was a wedding catalog. Aside from his work training soldiers at the camp, and his helping out here at Vance Ranch, Mac also was a wedding consultant on the side.

Lana typed on a keyboard with one hand. In the other, she held a steaming mug of coffee. The aroma of the beans tickled Rusty's nose as he approached. She didn't look up from her keyboard. He knew she was working on a story about the troubles veterans were having as they tried to reintegrate into civilian life.

"I hear you had a sleepover last night," said Mac. His brows waggled like a dastardly villain in a cartoon.

"It's Ronnie," said Rusty.

"Oh, good," said Lana looking up from her computer. "So, you guys are back together?"

Lana had met Ronnie a few times. The last time had been when Lana had stood Mac up for the wedding. Ronnie had missed the impromptu ceremony a few months ago that had taken place inside a bedroom after Lana climbed into the window.

"We're giving it another shot," said Rusty. At least that was the plan. This would be the negotiation of his life, and he was prepared to pull out all the stops to win his wife back. Just as soon as he found the one thing that would tear them apart.

"That's great, man." Mac clapped him on the back. "So, why don't you look thrilled? I thought this was what you wanted."

"It is. I am. I just—have you been in the bungalow recently?"

Both Mac and Lana shook their heads.

"I misplaced something important. An envelope. You haven't seen one laying around."

Again they both shook their heads.

"You hungry, Rusty?" Patty poked her head out of the screen door. Grizz filled the frame behind her. He rested his hand on her belly. When he did that, the small bump there became noticeable.

"No," said Rusty, eyes on the baby bump at Patty's midsection. "I'm just looking for something I lost. Have you seen an envelope laying around?"

The couple looked at each other and shook their heads.

It took Rusty a few minutes more to extricate himself from the two couples and their attempts to ply him with food or get details about Ronnie's return. Once he escaped, he turned and headed out to the pastures.

He found Brenda, Jules, and Romey in one of the fields spreading seed. Rusty knew the women were growing soybean plants on the pasture as a supplement to the cows' diet. What he marveled at was how the three lifelong enemies were getting along.

Brenda's hair was pulled back into a ponytail. Her green eyes sparkled as she laughed at something Jules said. Jules's hair was also pulled into a ponytail, but instead of straight strands, her hair was a collection of silky coils. Romey, whose hair was a riot of curls that stretched to the sun, shook her head at the laughing women.

"I can't believe the cows have taken to eating soy," said Brenda.

"Well, they're not our husbands," said Jules.

"In a way, our husbands are eating soybean," said Romey. "Since these are what the cattle consume."

"Hey, Rusty," said Brenda. "You looking for the guys? They headed over to the camp already."

"Actually, I wanted to talk to you, Bren. I misplaced an envelope sometime over the past few days. Have you seen anything laying around? Or," Rusty gulped, "been to the post office recently?"

"My brother was here the other day, and he took a bunch of mail to the post office."

Brenda's brother was a pastor. How ironic would that be if Pastor Vance was the one to dissolve Rusty's marriage.

CHAPTER EIGHT

*R*onnie stretched her limbs in the comfortable bed. Spread out like a starfish, her toes and fingertips weren't able to reach the four posts. It was luxurious.

She was used to sleeping alone. Rusty had been gone most months out of the year. What she wasn't used to was sleeping in sheets that didn't smell like her husband.

These sheets smelled like another man. They had the sweet tang of bacon on the pillow. She'd bet this had been David Porco's old room.

That was another thing she had missed about the separation from her husband. Military life, even though it came with all its trials and tribulations, came with a built-in tribe. No matter where she went, there was always a military family that would welcome her.

She'd particularly liked all of Rusty's team. From the ultra-organized Keaton to the broody Grizz, who she could talk poetry with. She'd missed the laughter of the prankster Mac. She'd missed explaining social nuances to Spinelli and steering her girlfriends away from Porco.

Ronnie might miss them, but she was surely using them. They were the subject of the next books she was writing. She'd planned a whole series featuring soldiers who would find their soul mates after their last deployment.

Each man would get his own story and a woman to compliment him. Spinelli would get a witty woman who could match his analytical mind. It would be funny if Porco got matched with a woman who was a vegetarian and didn't like bacon. For Mac, Ronnie wanted to write a second chance romance with the fiancée who'd stood him up. Grizz needed the girl next door type. Someone like Keaton's little sister Patty, who clearly was in love with him. Ronnie's biggest challenge was figuring out what kind of woman might ensnare the heart of Anthony Keaton. That woman would have to first snatch the checklists out of his hands and get him to look her in the eye. Ronnie wasn't sure such a strong woman existed.

The thought of giving those men love stories of their own after all they'd done to keep their country safe made Ronnie's heart fill. Unlike in the real world of military life, these books would be filled with long, lovey-dovey conversations where the calls didn't drop. There would be gifts in the mail that were delivered on an important date and not weeks or months later—or worse, not at all. There would be no wounds or injuries when the soldiers came home.

Ronnie knew she was writing a fairytale series. But no reader wanted to read the truth. The anxiety of waiting. The loneliness of long nights. The silence when a scheduled call was missed or didn't go through. The heartbreak when orders came that would separate loved ones and new friends over and over again.

No. None of that was romantic. So that's not what she wrote.

Ronnie pulled her laptop into the bed with her and began typing some more notes for the next story. An hour later, she looked up to see that it was approaching ten in the morning, nearing the time she and Rusty were due at the bank. She pulled on a robe as she padded around the bungalow, noting that Rusty wasn't at home.

He'd likely gone to work. No surprise there. She had no idea how the man planned to woo her back when he fell back into the same routines. At least he wasn't in any danger with his new job on the training camp. But it proved to her that he would never change.

His work had come before her when they were married. She'd signed up for that and knew she'd have to wait her turn. But when he'd taken on another assignment after they agreed he wouldn't reenlist, that had been the final straw.

The doorbell rang, jarring Ronnie out of her reverie. She tightened the robe around herself and went to open it. She expected one of the guys to be on the other side of the screen. Each man had spent time in their home when she and Rusty were married. Greeting them in a robe would be no big deal.

On the stoop stood a handsome man Ronnie had never seen before. When he lifted his head, she saw that there was a collar around his neck.

"Hi, I'm Pastor Vance."

Ronnie pulled the edges of her robe closer together. "I'm Veronica. Rusty's..."

"Wife?"

Standing in front of a pastor, wearing a robe, while in the home of a bachelor, Ronnie thought she should have felt vindicated by being called someone's wife. But instead, she grimaced. "Not for much longer."

The pastor's gaze swept down to her left hand, where she held her robe together. Pastor Vance wasn't leering at her. He was looking at her ring finger. Her left-hand ring finger to be exact. The one where a wedding ring should reside. All that was there was a tan line.

"Is Rusty here?" asked the pastor. "I seem to have collected a piece of mail that belongs to him. I would've mailed it for him, but there's no address."

"I'll take it." Ronnie took the long envelope from the man. She thought that was it, but the pastor lingered in the open door. "Is there something else you needed?"

"I have a habit of putting my nose in where it doesn't belong," he said, more to himself than to her. "I know the two of you are contemplating divorce. That's a big decision."

"I've already decided."

Pastor Vance's gaze was like lasers. His brows dipped, as though they were turning the knobs of his irises to focus. Did he see her lips tremble as she made the proclamation? Did he catch the wince at the edges of her eyes anytime she acknowledged the D-word?

"Rusty has sought counsel with me."

That surprised Ronnie. Rusty had never been a very religious man. She knew he believed in God, but he preferred to keep his own counsel rather than reach out to anyone else.

"I know he loves you very much."

Ronnie huffed. Everyone was constantly saying that. She knew Rusty loved her, intellectually. The problem was she could no longer feel that love.

"You don't believe that?" asked the pastor.

"I know he loves me. I love him, too. It's just not enough."

"What more do you want?"

"Passion. Romance."

"Ah."

"Let me guess." Ronnie let go of the edges of the robe to place her hands on her hips. "You think that's fanciful?"

"To the contrary," the pastor leaned against the door jam. "The Bible is filled with many romances. Adam and Eve, Abraham and Sarai, Isaac and

Rebekah. But the story I think is most apt to your situation is Jacob and Rachel."

Despite herself, Ronnie leaned in to listen to Pastor Vance's words. She was a sucker for a good story. And she did remember the story of Jacob and Rachel. It was the first Romeo and Juliet story, but instead of a balcony, Jacob had to toil in the fields for seven years to earn the hand of the woman he fell in love with. When it came time to reap his reward, Rachel's father played a trick on him.

"In the end, Jacob had to work twice as hard to win his lady love," the pastor was saying. "There is something romantic in hard work. To persevere through adversity shows passion. Don't you think?"

Rusty was a worthy man. Ronnie would never deny that. He had worked hard all these years. But he put more care into his career goals, working twice as hard at it than their relationship. At the end of the day, there was no passion left for her, no time for romance. And Ronnie knew that she needed those things to be happy.

"I think, Pastor Vance, that you're leaving out an important detail of that story. The first seven years Jacob worked, didn't he wind up marrying Rachel's older sister first?"

The pastor pursed his lips. "Well, there is that minor detail. But that wasn't the point."

"I think the point is that even if you work hard for something, it doesn't mean you'll get what you want in the end."

CHAPTER NINE

*R*usty looked in his rearview mirror for the twentieth time. Ronnie's car was still behind him. Not that he would miss Old Bessie. There was a cloud of smoke coming from her back end and the muffler that announced itself from a mile away.

Bessie had come with Ronnie into their wedding. Rusty had been trying to get rid of the old girl since right after the I do's. But Ronnie had insisted on keeping the gas-guzzling, Check Engine blinking, unreliable heap parked out front of the door.

At first, Rusty had grinned at her loyalty to the heap of oxidized metal. But after the third break down, one when he was overseas, he'd put his foot down and insisted on replacing the death trap with a newer model. Rusty decided patience would be the avenue to take to get rid of the old jalopy.

The joke was on him. His soon to be ex-wife sat comfortably on the exposed springs in Old Bessie's driver's seat. Meanwhile, Rusty was the one looking at them both in his rearview mirror.

Ronnie had insisted on driving herself to the bank. She'd always been an independent woman. That was something Rusty had loved about her. She'd come from a large family, where he'd been an only child. His independence had come naturally where Ronnie had had to fight for every morsel of solitude and autonomy she could come by.

He'd thought that had been a strength in their union; that she didn't mind being left alone. For five years, he'd given her the peace and quiet she'd craved. He'd bought her an eReader and had never once balked at the monthly credit card bill when there was always an extra digit beside bookstore charges. Those charges were often more than the electric or gas bill. But if it kept his wife happy, he was happy to do it.

Rusty had given her everything she wanted. And he still had no clue why she was walking away from him. Or rather, lagging behind him.

He'd slowed his speed to allow her to catch up

with him. Yet, she kept letting others pass between them. Keeping at least a car length or two between them.

Rusty took a left turn into the bank's parking lot. Cutting his engine, he waited for Ronnie to park her car beside his. Old Bessie grumbled and growled as she came into the lot. Ronnie pulled into the farthest spot. Rusty jogged over to the old Chevy in time to be there to open the door for her, but he was too late.

Veronica gave the metal door a shove. It squeaked on its ancient hinges, as though it were loathe to give her up. Rusty couldn't blame the old beast.

Ronnie stepped out in a sundress. The yellow of the garment made her skin shine brighter than the sun. Her normally wild hair was tamed back into a bun atop her head, but a few tendrils rebelled and curled around her neck. Rusty couldn't take his gaze off the hem of the dress, which brushed her knees. His fingers clenched with each swish as she walked toward him.

"You got everything you need?" Ronnie asked.

No, he didn't have everything he needed. He didn't have the one thing he knew he needed in his life. The only thing he needed was her. The woman he loved was standing in front of him, within arms distance, and he couldn't touch her.

He couldn't say that. So, he nodded.

He couldn't touch her either. So, he waved his hand for Ronnie to proceed into the bank.

As Rusty stepped into the establishment, his training kicked in. His eyes scanned for tactical weaknesses and advantages. The glass door closing behind him was the only entrance. Though he assumed there would be another exit behind where the tellers worked. There was only one security camera. But the red light to indicate that the device was on was blank. Meaning it was either out of service or someone had forgotten to turn it on.

This place would be a robber's paradise. But not in this town. Of course, there were a few bad apples in the community. There were in every community. But in a town where everyone knew everyone else, crime wasn't a booming business due to the lack of anonymity.

Still, Rusty was ever vigilant. His most prized treasure was inside these four walls. He shadowed Ronnie as they waited in the reception area for their appointed time.

There was a small line inside the bank for the tellers. There was no glass partition separating tellers from their customers like in most cities. A bowl of lollipops sat in front of both of the two tellers. They smiled when the adults took the candies at the conclusion of their business.

A new adult stepped into the bank. This man didn't look like he had two pennies to rub together. His hair was a bird's nest. His clothes were wrinkled, and his sneakers caked with mud that smelled rancid, as though he'd just walked through a horse stall.

The tension fairly crackled in the air when the tellers became aware of him. Rusty edged his body closer to Ronnie, who appeared oblivious. She was thumbing through the documents in her bag.

The man walked up to the teller and leaned into the counter. "I need my money."

His hands were empty. There was no bulge in his waistband, meaning he likely wasn't armed. Still, Rusty stayed alert.

"Do you have an account with us, sir?"

The man sighed. He pinched the bridge of his nose as though a headache pained him. "My wife takes care of the paperwork. She left me because I couldn't get the money."

"I'm sorry for your financial woes, sir. But I don't think we can do anything about that."

The man released the hold he had on his nose and slammed his hand down on the counter. The teller jumped. Ronnie finally looked up.

"Something's wrong with my head," he said. "They don't believe me, so they won't give me the money."

"I'm sorry—" The teller began but didn't finish.

The man turned on his muddied heel and stormed out of the bank. He flashed Rusty a look as he went out the door. Rusty stared at the closed door for a few moments, making certain the man didn't come back inside. The tellers were in a tizzy during that time but soon settled. That scene might play out more regularly in a big city, but he was certain it was an anomaly in such a small town.

"Mr. and Mrs. Hook?"

Rusty's heart kicked up at those words, the homeless man all but forgotten. This would likely be the last time he'd hear Ronnie called that. A thorough search of the ranch had not produced the missing divorce papers. Pastor Vance hadn't answered the phone when Rusty had called the church earlier.

Beside him, Ronnie bristled at the title, but she gave a curt nod of her head to the short man with spectacles that approached them. He had a few wisps on his balding head. The buttons on his suit strained to keep his belly contained as he reached out his hand to Rusty.

"I'm Mr. Denton, the bank manager." Mr. Denton's handshake was clammy. He winced as Rusty's hands gripped his and squeezed. The man rearranged his features to smile at Ronnie.

Ronnie offered her hand, but Mr. Denton was already turning into his office. He swept his hand in front of his paunch, indicating that Ronnie precede the men. Ronnie's hand dropped to her side, and she stepped in and sat.

"What's this loan for?" Mr. Denton asked, his gaze fixed on Rusty as he spoke. "A new home? Are you expecting a new addition soon?"

Rusty's tongue tied when he tried to speak. He had trouble forming the single syllabic word that would answer that statement. Because more than anything, he wished it could be true.

"No," said Ronnie. The two lettered word settled like a bomb going off. The shrapnel tore at Rusty's insides. "It's for a business loan."

"Oh," Mr. Denton grinned. "What kind of business are you getting into, son?"

Denton pulled out a stack of clipped papers and

sat them on the desk before Rusty. Then he grabbed a heavy-looking pen and clicked it open.

Rusty could feel the heat rolling off of Ronnie. During his time overseas, he'd had to hold his tongue as men spoke for women who clearly had other ideas. The tide of cultural change was slowly shifting in the Middle East. It had turned decades ago here on his home turf. Perhaps Mr. Denton hadn't gotten the memo?

"*I...*" Ronnie said the single word pointedly, letting it draw out until Mr. Denton turned his attention to her. "...am going into publishing."

The banker looked from Ronnie to Rusty. His thick brows pushed together in confusion. After a moment, they separated as though understanding dawned. "Have you written a cookbook, my dear?"

Rusty had neither the time nor luxury for the grimace that threatened. He sat forward, blocking Ronnie from the man who had painted a black and white bull's eye just above the bridge of his nose.

"My wife is a brilliant storyteller," said Rusty.

That was pretty much all he could say. Ronnie always wove the most fantastic of tales when she lay in his arms at night. Or when the phone line between them had a good connection. Listening to her simply tell him about her day drowned out the noise of the combat zone outside.

"Fiction books?" said Mr. Denton, his brows pulling together again to mark the target on his forehead. "Oh, well, I'm sure it's not one of those bare-chested books in the grocery store. Can you believe they have the audacity to sell that smut where kids can see them?"

"Did you know that romance books are a billion-dollar industry?" said Ronnie. "There are women all over this nation making living wages, or more, and supporting their families off of writing those love stories."

"Is that what you've written?" The banker screwed up his nose. "A romance novel?"

Ronnie swallowed and bit her lip.

Mr. Denton put down his pen and began pulling the documents back to himself.

"What I wrote…" Ronnie began, then stopped. She licked her lips as though she were making a decision about something. "It's about life in the military through a wife's perspective."

The banker's gaze brightened. He slid the paperwork back on the desk. "That sounds remarkable. An excellent way to support your husband in his endeavors."

Ronnie pursed her lips together and kept her mouth shut for the rest of the meeting. It wasn't like her, and Rusty wanted to know why. More importantly, he wanted to get his hands on the book she'd written. Maybe it would provide some clues as to what had gone wrong in their marriage and how he could fix it.

CHAPTER TEN

The check in her hand didn't feel as freeing as she'd thought. She slipped it into her canvas bag. Inside that canvas bag, Ronnie had prepared documents and charts. She had research about how the romance industry was indeed a billion dollar a year industry. She had printouts of success stories of women like Norah Roberts, Debbie Macomber, and her favorite, Robyn Carr. All housewives who had made a career of writing those books Mr. Denton had sneered at.

Robyn Carr was Ronnie's idol. Because just like Ronnie, Mrs. Carr had been a military wife. She'd traveled from base to base, never staying anywhere too long, but carrying a romance novel as her best company. When Carr put pen to paper, she created a world that warmed the hearts of millions.

Those success stories were nothing to sniff at. But that's what most men did. Some women, too, as evidenced by Ronnie's waitress the other day.

Romance novels were a viable and respectable industry. So why hadn't she admitted that was the business this check was going to fund? Why hadn't she spoken up when Mr. Denton had put it down?

"You know, I'd love to read your book when it's ready."

Ronnie jerked at the sound of Rusty's voice. He was standing outside her car door, leaning against the hood. They'd arrived back at the ranch. Rusty had trailed behind her as she'd driven Old Bessie. She'd seen him through the puffs of smoke Bessie blew back at him as they cruised down the streets.

"It still needs work." Ronnie fidgeted with the keys. Her gaze darted to the canvas bag, where the mock-up of the first draft of her book sat.

She'd brought the prototype to the loan meeting. But she was glad she hadn't taken it out of the bag. The guy on the cover wasn't exactly bare-chested. He had on a shirt. But it had a few buttons open. She was certain if stuffy old Denton had seen it, he'd shove the loan documents back in his desk and show them the door.

Ronnie cut the ignition. As she yanked the key out, the car let out a huff of air that mirrored her emotions. She gave the steering wheel a pat of commiseration before stepping out of the vehicle.

"When's the last time you took her to a mechanic?" asked Rusty.

"Bessie's fine."

"She's coughing up fumes, which for a human means a symptom of sickness. She needs to see a doctor, which for a car is a mechanic."

"You got me the loan, Rusty," she snapped, rounding on him. "The health of my car is not your concern."

Rusty let out a long, weary sigh through his nose. His features were strained, but Ronnie could tell he was pulling for patience. He never used to do that with her.

When they were first married, there had always been a light in his eyes when he'd looked at her. Like the sun rose and set on her face. For the past year, when they spoke, he'd eyed her warily, as though he were waiting for her to pull down a shade of darkness between them.

"Even though we're not married anymore," he said, "I'm always going to be concerned about you."

Rusty stood directly in front of the sun. She wanted to shade her eyes as she looked up at him. She felt the darkness prickle at the back of her neck.

"We are still married," she said, surprised to hear the tremble of need in her voice. "For now, that is. Until you sign the divorce papers."

A flicker went across his features. Ronnie couldn't tell if it was defiance or defeat? The thought of the first emotion raised her ire. The thought of the latter emotion made her shiver.

"Seven days," he said. "You said you'd stay for a week, and then I'll sign."

Rusty's voice was monotone as he spoke, lifeless. It sounded like a threat when he said it this time. It sounded as though he was leaving her now. The thought settled like acid in the pit of her stomach.

"Seven days," she repeated. "And then you'll sign."

"You have my word."

Ronnie nodded. She turned from him, taking a step toward the bungalow. But Rusty's hand fell to the small of her back. When it did, a weight settled inside of her. Something that had been out of place clicked back into its spot.

"Why don't you come up to the main house," said Rusty. "You didn't get a chance to say hi to the guys. They want to see you. They want you to meet their wives."

Ronnie hesitated. Her life as a military wife had been a revolving door of new people every few months. Finding a friend that she connected within the last couple of weeks of being stationed at a base, only to have them leave or Rusty get new orders and then lose touch. She wanted off that roller coaster. She wanted roots where people stayed put, and no one would leave in the middle of the night.

She stepped away from Rusty's hand. They were only separated by a foot, but she felt like she was free falling. "I'm tired after today. I'm just gonna go and lay down for a bit and then get to work."

"On your romance novel?"

She should've known he'd figure it out. Ronnie had bought her fair share of bare-chested covers during their marriage. She'd never left them out for Rusty to see. Or so she thought. Clearly, she hadn't been as careful with her reading materials as she'd thought.

"Don't start."

Rusty held up his hands. "I wasn't going to. You

made some good points back there at the bank. It sounds like you've researched this business."

Had she heard a note of derision in how he said the word business? Rusty had never commented on her reading material before. He'd never snatched a bodice ripper from her hands like others had.

"But if it's about us, I would like to read it?"

"It's not about us," she insisted.

"Military wife?"

"There are thousands of military wives in the world."

"You were always amazing at weaving stories and tales," he said as though he didn't hear her. "Maybe if I read your book, I can finally figure out what I did wrong."

"You didn't do anything wrong, Russ."

"Then why aren't you in my arms right now?"

Ronnie didn't miss the hint of anger in his voice. She had no words to answer the bewilderment in his eyes.

"Why did we fail, Ronnie?"

She pursed her lips. She'd never been able to vocalize what had gone wrong between them. All she could ever tell him was that something was missing. She'd thought that missing piece had been him. But here he was, standing in front of her. And like he said, she wasn't in his arms.

"I thought we were fine."

"Of course, you thought that. You were never there."

"I was out building a life for us."

"I was at home living a life without you."

"Is there someone else?"

Ronnie's gaze went wide. "Is that what you think of me?"

"I don't know what to think?" Rusty raked his fingers through his hair. It had grown long now that he was out of the military. "One day, things are fine, and the next, you're shoving papers in my face and telling me you don't want me in your life."

"I never said I didn't want you in my life."

"Well, that's what happens when people get divorced. It's a dissolution. A separation of two things that are no longer connected."

That's what she wanted, right? To be separate from him. To be apart from him. To be on her own. That's what she'd felt all these years. But the thought of not seeing him again, ever, terrified her.

Ronnie looked at Rusty's hands. Those strong capable hands that had always grounded her. When he'd touched her, she'd felt rooted again, like the tree she'd always climb and read her books in. He was keeping his distance now. Which was what she wanted, right?

"I've only ever tried to give you what you wanted," Rusty said, exhaustion in his voice. "I just don't know what that is anymore. And I'm not sure you do either."

Ronnie steeled herself for a long argument. One where he kept her talking, using his negotiating tactics to try and determine a way past her defenses. One where he made it seem like he was acquiescing to her every demand, only to see that he'd played her right into his hand.

Rusty clamped his mouth shut. He turned on his heel and walked away from her. Leaving Ronnie alone as the sky above her began to darken.

CHAPTER ELEVEN

*R*usty stomped on the jack. Old Bessie's big, clunky body raised inch by inch as though she were reluctant to expose her underbelly. With the car sufficiently jacked up, Rusty grabbed his tools, slid under the behemoth, and got to work.

He was greeted by the sight of rusty pipes. Lubricants wouldn't work to smooth things over with this muffler. It was welded to the rusted pipes and would need to be hacked off.

Great.

Rusty grabbed for his hacksaw and began cutting into the faulty piece of hardware. The sound of metal banging against metal wore off the last vestiges of his anger. No, anger was the wrong word for what he felt.

Frustration was more like it. And a healthy heaping of confusion.

Rusty wasn't used to facing a problem he couldn't solve. The United States Military had invested too much into his training to ensure that he was well equipped to deal with any negotiation matters that came before him. But in none of his textbooks had he ever come across how to deal with women.

More times than not, men were the hostage-takers in the theater of war. Males were also more likely than women to take their own lives in crisis situations. The most used tactic during these confrontations was to get the hostile to talk. Talking, and airing out their feelings, is not what most men are known for. Still, more often than not, the strategy worked.

Rusty had talked people down from high ledges. He'd talked them out of suicide vests. He'd talked them into releasing hostages. The problem was that he was the hostage in this situation with Ronnie. And he'd developed Stockholm Syndrome.

Ronnie had stolen his heart the first time he'd laid eyes on her wild hair. He hadn't seen her eyes as her head had been buried between the covers of a book. When she'd lowered the book, his world had tilted. She could've hog-tied him and carted him off then and there. She'd captured his attention, and he didn't want to be let go.

The problem was Ronnie was all too ready to let him go. She'd been cutting all ties to him for the past year. Rusty had tried to tighten the knots, but no matter how hard he pulled them, the binds wouldn't hold.

Using the wrench, he tightened the bolts on the new muffler. Its smooth face looked out of place amidst the dirt and grime of Bessie's underbelly. She clearly needed an oil change. And the front tires were low on air.

The car was a death trap waiting for a bump in the road to take it down. Had Ronnie been driving this hunk of metal like this without any maintenance or repair since the last time he'd seen her? She never let mechanics touch it because they'd tell her the truth; that the car should go to the junkyard in the sky.

Rusty had always done the maintenance himself under the cover of night when he was home. When he wasn't home, he'd always made sure a buddy checked on the state of the car for him. He knew Ronnie had been staying with her parents for the last few months, so he'd had no way of checking to see if her Check Engine light was on.

He slid from under the car. After releasing the jack, he pulled open the driver's side door. He still had a spare key. He used it to start the engine up.

Old Bessie purred, like a cat who'd just had a good belly rub. No smoke or grumbles came from the rear of the car. The Check Engine light didn't turn on either.

That was a small blessing. It still left the tires to be replaced, and the oil changed. He wondered if he'd have time to tend to that maintenance before she woke up.

Here he only had a few days left to talk her back into being his wife, and he'd spent all morning fixing her car. But he didn't know what else to do? He didn't know what to say to her? Not a single page from any of his training manuals would help him.

Rusty rubbed a hand across his forehead. The back of his hand slicked quickly across his flesh. He turned his hand over to see that there was grease on his knuckles. There was grime on his shirt.

He yanked the shirt over his head. Turning it inside out, he wiped the grime from his head and headed around the car. He opened the passenger door to set the seats right again when a book fell out.

The paperback landed in the dirt, just shy of an oil spill. Rusty reached out and rescued the book before the cover could be spoiled. Ronnie regarded books as precious items that should be set up high. Using his shirt, he brushed the dirt from the cover. What he found beneath the thin layer of grime perplexed him.

The book featured a nearly bare-chested man clutching a woman on the cover. The pose was on the provocative side. But not much racier than anything he'd seen on the grocery store shelves next to magazines.

Grocery store shelves? Rusty heard the stuffy banker's voice in his head. He remembered Ronnie's shoulders bristle with tension at the man's words. Rusty couldn't understand why? It wasn't like she read any of those bodice ripper books.

In their home, the shelves had been lined with the classics. He'd often catch Ronnie reading two books at a time. One inside the other, in fact.

Rusty's eyes scanned away from the indecent couple and caught the title of the book. *Seduced by the Sergeant* was written in a bright, curly script that hurt his eyes. The title was in stark contrast to the jewel tones surrounding the couple.

His eyes quickly darted away from those words

down to the bottom of the book. There he found the author's name; V.E. O'Brian

V? E? It couldn't be. But they were. Those were Ronnie's initials; Veronica Elizabeth. O'Brian was her maiden name.

V.E. O'Brian. That was her. This was Ronnie's book.

Rusty's hands shook as he held the book in his palms. It felt like a bomb. A slight wind blew, rustling the pages. The rustling sounded like a bomb ticking down to an explosion.

He should put the book down. Carefully. He should step away. Slowly.

Rusty opened the covers to a random page and read the first line he saw.

Ryker pulled her close, smashing her tender bosom against his rock hard chest. Vanessa struggled in his hold, but it was no use. She was helpless to escape the sergeant's captivity.

"Let me go," Vanessa pleaded.

"Your pretty mouth says no," Ryker growled. "But your lush body says yes."

His lips crashed down to hers in a brutal claiming. Vanessa felt as though she were being pulled under by his passion. Never had she experienced such a sensation. She wanted more. But she couldn't-

"Rusty?"

Rusty slammed the covers of the book closed and pressed it to his chest. He turned his head to look over his shoulder.

Veronica stood at the door to the house. Her gaze wasn't on him. It was on the back end of her car. With her attention diverted, Rusty took the opportunity to wrap the book in his shirt.

"What are you doing to my car?"

"I fixed the muffler."

Ronnie frowned. Her head snapped to him. Ire was bright in her gaze. But as her eyes dipped to his bare chest, the look in her eyes softened. Rusty saw when she caught herself looking. Her lips pressed together, and her gaze shuttered.

"I didn't ask you to do that," she huffed.

"Just because we're not together anymore doesn't mean I'm not going to concern myself with your safety."

"I can handle my own car maintenance."

"Yeah, your mouth is saying one thing, but your actions say something else entirely."

Her eyes flashed up at him. A tiny breath escaped her mouth. Rusty had seen that expression many times. It typically led to her coming into his embrace for long, luxurious moments of kissing.

Ronnie blinked and gave herself a shake. But even as she walked to the driver's side door, she seemed flustered. "I'm heading into town to run some errands."

"You'll be back for dinner."

Ronnie's hand froze on the driver's side door handle. Her gaze rose to his. There hadn't been a question in his statement. It was more of a command.

Rusty was ready to open his mouth and take it all back when she swallowed. Her lip trembled as she bobbed her head and then disappeared into the interior of the car.

Rusty said nothing as he watched her go. Once Ronnie and the old Chevy were ambling quietly down the drive, he pulled out the book. Unwrapping it from his shirt, he peered down at the garish cover.

She had written those words. He'd just used them against her. Maybe this was the text he'd been looking for; the negotiation tactics he'd need to win back his wife? With the book in hand, Rusty headed round the back of the house and started studying the first page.

CHAPTER TWELVE

*R*onnie took the long road into town in silence. Complete and utter silence. Bessie didn't grunt or grumble once after she pulled away from the ranch. The only sound that rang out in the car was the sound of Rusty's voice in Ronnie's mind.

Yeah, your mouth is saying one thing, but your actions say something else entirely.

He'd never spoken to her like that. Sure, she'd heard him speak like that to others. To men and women who were below him in rank. There had been many phone calls she'd overheard or times on base when she'd happened by her Rusty giving orders.

In fact, the first time they'd met, she'd

remembered he'd taken that tone with someone. She'd been reading a book about a pirate and a lady he'd absconded with. Rusty's deep baritone had made her heart kick in her chest and brought her head up from reading her book. It was his friendly smile and his gentlemanly manners that held her attention.

You'll be back for dinner, he'd commanded. Demanded.

Just exactly who did he think he was? He certainly wasn't the boss of her. If Rusty thought he could give her orders, he had another thought coming.

Though there had been something about the timbre in his voice. It sent a shiver over her shoulders just thinking about it.

In fact, it made her think of another man. It made her think of Sergeant Ryker Catch from her novel. That was exactly something he would say to the heroine Vanessa. Right before he swept her off her feet and into a heated kiss.

Rusty wasn't that type of man. He didn't have Ryker's devil-may-care attitude. Rusty would only ever pick a woman up if she was in danger, and after he had her express consent and permission to handle her body in such an intimate fashion.

Chivalry wasn't dead. It was just bogged down and knotted up in a mess of political correctness and changing cultural norms.

Ronnie shook the memory off of Rusty's words and their effects. It was anger she'd heard in his voice. Rusty was still upset that she wanted the divorce. But there was nothing he could do— certainly not in five days—to change her mind.

The car ride into town was smooth. He'd not only fixed the muffler, he'd reset her seat back into its prime position, a feat Ronnie had had trouble with. Now the car cradled her low back. It was the same feeling as when Rusty splayed his hand on her low back, that feeling of being rooted.

That was Rusty. He sprouted roots, where she wanted adventure. He was good for fixing her car, fixing things around the house. Practical things. Not the romantic things she wrote about. There were no candlelight dinners, or long walks, or gazing into each other's eyes.

There were Skype calls in low lighting. There were long stretches of silence when he was on a mission. There were always other people in the background when they did have a strong enough connection to see each other.

Ronnie had thought she had what it took to be a

military wife. But she'd been wrong. She knew Rusty was no longer in the service, but she also knew that hadn't been the plan. He'd planned to serve at least another five years. She never would've lasted that long. She was certain as soon as the divorce papers were signed, he'd sign right back up for the service.

Putting the car in park, Ronnie tugged her satchel out of the passenger side of the car. She had a long to-do list today. At the top of the list was to find a photographer and cover model for her book. Now that she had the money, she didn't have to rely on stock photos.

The smells of fried foods and slow-cooking soups greeted her nose as she stepped out of the car. Ronnie's gaze immediately swung back to the Mexican restaurant she'd visited the other day. Though her roots were Irish, her tastebuds thought they were from the south of the U.S. border.

Stepping through the entryway, Ronnie sidled up to a booth inside the taco joint. She made sure to choose an area different from the first one she'd sat in the other day. She hoped she wouldn't see the judgy waitress from her first meal here.

An older couple sat across from her. Their brown skin was wrinkled, but there was a youthful look to the both of them. The woman wore a colorful sari clueing Ronnie in that their ancestry was from India. Looking closely at the man, Ronnie realized she recognized him. He was the doctor who had tended to Russell after his fall.

Dr. Patel held his wife's hands, grinning like a wolf. Mrs. Patel looked down demurely, then up through thick eyelashes. Adoration and love was clear on their faces

Marla, the waitress from the other day, stepped up to the Patels's table. "Here's the check, Pastor Patel."

"Oh, no," said Mrs. Patel as she snatched the slip of paper away from her husband. "I invited this handsome devil on this date, so I'm paying. Unfortunately, for me, he's not a cheap date."

"No," chuckled Dr. Patel, "but I'm worth it, my darling."

"Yes, that you are."

Pastor Patel kissed his wife's knuckles. "You'll forgive me that I don't see you home. I have to get back to work."

"As long as you're home by dinner. No more late nights. You promised."

"I will rush home to be with you before the sun sets." Dr. Patel bent down and kissed his wife's temple. When he straightened, his gaze caught Ronnie's. "Mrs. Hook, how nice to see you again."

Ronnie hadn't been called Mrs. Hook in a long time. It had been a running joke with her and Rusty, where she imagined herself as Wendy married to the pirate.

"Hello, Dr. Patel. Or is it Pastor?"

"I am both," he said. "This is my wife. Deeksha, this is Russell Hook's wife."

"Lovely to meet you, my dear," said Mrs. Patel. "Your husband is such a kind soul."

Ronnie decided not to correct the older couple on her marital status. Besides, she was right. Rusty was a kind soul. His manners weren't why she wanted a divorce. His long absences and shortcomings in the romance department were.

Dr. Patel gave his wife another wave as he walked out of the door. But Mrs. Patel wasn't eyeing her husband. Her gaze was trained on Ronnie's computer screen, where bare-chested men were on display.

Ronnie decided that was the perfect time to come clean about her marital status. "Russell and I are separated."

"Is that a dating site?" asked Mrs. Patel.

"No, I'm not dating." The very idea of dating

another man didn't appeal to Ronnie. From now on, she preferred to keep men between the covers of a book rather than step out onto a real-world stage. "I'm looking for a cover model."

"Are you a writer?"

"I am."

"Let me guess; romance novels?"

Ronnie searched the woman's gaze for judgment. When she found none, she answered tentatively, "Yes."

"I love romance novels," sighed Mrs. Patel.

"You're a pastor's wife."

That came from Marla. Ronnie had forgotten the woman was nearby. Marla turned from the table she'd been bussing with raised brows. What Ronnie didn't understand was why Marla's brows were raised at her and not the pastor's wife.

"There are many love stories in the Bible," said Mrs. Patel.

Marla sniffed at that, looking anything but cowed.

Ronnie hoped Mrs. Patel wouldn't pull out any examples. She'd already had this discussion with Pastor Vance, and happily-ever-afters hadn't faired so well with the biblical characters.

"But I prefer the more contemporary tales," Mrs.

Patel continued. "I especially love the ones with the males who shift into wolves." She giggled like a schoolgirl. "Do you write those?"

"No," said Ronnie. "I write military romances."

"Fitting, since your husband is in the military."

Ronnie wanted to balk at that. Her books were not based on her life with Rusty. Sure, the hero was a soldier. And sure, a lot of the book had the hero and heroine separated with him off fighting. And maybe her heroine was a writer. But that was where the similarities ended.

"Mrs. Patel," said Marla. "I had no idea you read smut."

"Smut?" said Mrs. Patel. "Romance novels are far from smut. They are about women's empowerment. The modern love story is the one where women are the heroes of their own stories. These tales deal with women's issues, women's goals, their growth, and their pleasure."

"B-but," sputtered the waitress. "But they set unrealistic expectations for young girls."

"Unrealistic, how?" asked Mrs. Patel.

"They're not about real men," said Marla. "No real man in this world knows the first thing about romance. The women who read these will face disappointment all their lives if they believe such nonsense."

Ronnie had been Team Mrs. Patel for the duration of the discussion. Now she was torn. Marla made a good point. The men in romance novels were figments of women's imagination. Even she knew that as she penned her hero. She knew Rusty would never behave the same way that Ryker would.

"If it's romance that you want," said Mrs. Patel, "then you need to tell your partner. You can't expect him to know. You have to show him, which is why sometimes I take my husband out on dates so he can know what I like."

Now it was Ronnie and Marla who shared a disbelieving look. Tell a man what you want? And then expect him to deliver? That was a true fantasy!

CHAPTER THIRTEEN

"*I*s this what women want?" Rusty pointed to the book on the console. The spine of the tome cracked in answer as he pressed the splayed pages open. Though Rusty wasn't sure if the crackling sound was a resounding no or a heartfelt yes?

The men who looked over his shoulder made grunting sounds and coughs. Again, Rusty was unsure if their unintelligible words were in agreement or discord. For his entire career as a hostage negotiator, he had been the talker in the group, the one with the answers. It was the first time he was at a loss for words.

"'*Ryker used his powerful forearm to swipe the romantic dinner off the floor*,'" read Keaton. His no-

nonsense tone was at odds with the words from Ronnie's book. "*He scooped Vanessa up to his powerful chest—*"

"You shouldn't use the same word twice in the same paragraph," Spinelli spoke up. "It sounds repetitive and leads to the reader's dissatisfaction."

"*He scooped Vanessa up to his powerful chest and took her mouth against his. Vanessa struggled against him but soon realized the fight was futile. He was right; she did want this. There was nothing more for her to do. His strength was more powerful than hers.*"

"That's the third time." Spinelli held up a finger. "What? She used powerful three times. She needs an editor. Or a thesaurus."

"*His strength was more powerful than hers. Ryker was going to take her.*"

That was the end of the chapter. Keaton didn't turn the page. They all knew what would happen next.

"What happens next?" asked Spinelli. "Where is he taking her?"

Keaton and Rusty shared a look.

"He's taking her upstairs," said Keaton.

"For what?" said Spinelli. "Who's going to clean up that mess they just made?"

Rusty didn't bother trying to explain. Spinelli

had a habit of taking things very literally, and Rusty didn't want to go any further down that road with the man. Besides, he still hadn't had his first question answered.

"Do women really want that?" he asked. "Do they want a man to, well, manhandle them? Do they want him to take charge and not seek any of her input? Do they want to be dominated like this?"

Rusty would never think of pulling Ronnie to him and kissing her if she'd turned away from him. But the inner monologue of her heroine didn't protest when the hero's powerful lips met hers. In real life, Ryker Catch's actions would be considered sexual harassment, possibly even assault.

Except the Vanessa character was consenting. Consenting in her mind. But how was a man to know that? Why didn't she just come out and say that that's what she wanted?

"It seems like these are the character's inner wishes," said Spinelli.

The man wasn't great at reading emotions. He was far more analytical. But he had a point.

"It gives a checklist of how to woo a woman who wants to be wooed but says she doesn't," said Keaton. "I'm glad Brenda just comes on out and tells me what she wants."

Rusty did envy his friend that. Brenda Vance Keaton was a no-nonsense woman who always said what she meant. She had to be. She bossed a whole ranch of men around.

Spinelli's wife, Romey, was also pretty straightforward when she spoke. Romey was a scientist, used to data and measurements. So she had to be exact when she spoke.

Ronnie had always had her head buried in books. She often had a pile of books around her and would read more than one at a time. Words were like a buffet for her. She wanted to use them all, even if she seemed to get stuck on the word *powerful*.

"Though sometimes it feels as though Brenda wants me to guess," said Keaton, peering closer at the book.

"I wish I knew what Romey was thinking when she gets quiet," said Spinelli, also leaning in to focus on the words on the page.

"Maybe we should keep reading," said Keaton, already making a note on his checklist.

Rusty turned the page to the next chapter, and there was that word again. *Vanessa lay her hand against Ryker's bare chest. His heart beat* powerfully.

Powerful. Should Rusty be more powerful in his relationship with her? He'd tried to be accommodating for the last few months. He'd tried to figure out what it was that she needed so that he could provide that for her.

Ronnie had said she wanted more romance in their life. But was this it? In this book, the heroine was constantly getting put into danger, which the hero would rescue her from. Rusty spent his career trying to ensure the world was a safer place for not only his countrymen but for his wife. He was not about to put Ronnie in harm's way.

"I suppose I could do a candlelight dinner," Rusty said, noting the elements of the scene they'd just read.

"You should do the part where he buys her clothes," said Keaton, bringing up how the previous scene in the novel had started.

The Ryker character had brought Vanessa a designer gown. Though how the man could afford such an expensive piece of clothing on a soldier's salary was beyond Rusty. The man also lived in a mansion and seemed to have a lot of leisure time between his missions, both falsehoods. But this was her fantasy.

This was her fantasy? That a powerful man would make her dinner, and buy her clothes, and spirit her away to his huge house, and spend free time he shouldn't have with her. This was Ronnie's fantasy. This was what she wanted.

"What about the part where she's in danger?" said Keaton.

In the next chapter, where they are upstairs, and Ryker was kissing Vanessa *powerfully*, the bad guys from Ryker's last mission burst into the house and interrupt the amorous activities. Never mind that ten known insurgents would never make it out of the deserts, past Homeland Security, and into a major U.S. city.

"How can you replicate that?" asked Keaton.

"You could stage a home invasion during the romantic dinner," said Spinelli.

It seemed like a lot, but Rusty was willing to try. He was willing to do anything to get his wife back. If dinner and danger were what she wanted, then that's what she was going to get.

"Oh, and wear a suit," said Keaton.

"A suit? I don't have a suit. I only have my military uniform."

"Chicks dig the uniform," said Keaton.

Rusty gave a sigh. A willing sigh. He had a lot of work ahead of him before Ronnie got home tonight. But if all went well, maybe she would realize he could give her exactly what she wanted.

CHAPTER FOURTEEN

*R*onnie could hear the laughter from the big house before she turned off the engine to her car. She saw the group roaming around on the big porch. They were all smiles. Most of the faces were familiar.

Grizz was the first familiar form she recognized. It was hard not to. The man was the size of a bear. Resting against his large form was a small woman. The flaming red hair marked the woman as Patricia Keaton.

Ronnie had seen the attraction between the two the times she'd visited the Keatons for holidays. Grizz had tried to keep his distance from his best friend's baby sister, but like a perfectly plotted romance novel, little Patty had gone and bagged herself a bear of a man. Ronnie made a mental note for the next characters in her book to use elements of this love story.

Sneaking an embrace as they came up the steps were Mac and Lana. Ronnie had worried if the two would ever make it down the aisle, but it looked like they had. Not that Ronnie was surprised. The no-nonsense journalist and the romantic wedding planner were exact opposites, making them the perfect foils for each other.

Though they hadn't always been in constant contact, those four had been constants in Ronnie's life when the whole team gathered. But she wasn't part of the team anymore. She was the one who'd left this time.

She'd be leaving again soon. But the next place she settled, Ronnie was determined to grow roots. She would find her forever home and her forever friends that she would keep for the rest of her life.

Turning away from the friends of her past, Ronnie trudged up to the front door of the bungalow. The door was unlocked. Of course, it was. This was a ranch filled with military men who had signed up to give their lives for their country. Of course, they would do tenfold for their loved ones. Only an idiot would dare trespass on this land.

Inside, the house was dark. But a glow from the dining room caught Ronnie's gaze. She headed in that direction, lulled by a peculiar scent.

In the small, candlelit dining room stood Rusty. He was decked out in full military regalia. At first, Ronnie took in the delectable sight of him.

Russell Hook had always filled out that uniform nicely. The gold buttons down his torso highlighted the sparkle in his eyes. The floppy cap on his head took away some of the seriousness of the ensemble

She had always loved seeing him fully decked out like this. But those times were few and far between. Mostly when…

"Oh, no," Ronnie dropped her canvas bag and rushed to him. "Who died?"

"Died?" Rusty had been grinning. But that cocky look dissipated from his features. "No one died."

"But you're in your full uniform. You only wear that when you've lost a soldier."

Rusty let out a weary sigh and looked skyward. "I didn't think of that."

His gaze fell past her and looked off to the side. Ronnie followed his gaze down to the dining room table. An elegant tablecloth was laid on the scratched wood surface. The candlelight that had led her in here cast a glow on the spread of her favorite foods.

"No one died," said Rusty. "I made you a special dinner."

"You made this?"

"I had it delivered."

There was a veritable Mexican buffet on the table. Rice, beans, queso, and guacamole. The spices of peppers and cilantro filled the air.

"Mexican's still your favorite, yeah?"

"Yeah."

Ronnie's stomach grumbled with want. She'd just had a burrito for lunch. Her stomach appeared to have quickly forgotten that meal and was ready for another.

"And I brought you this."

Rusty held up a gown. It was unlike anything Ronnie would've bought for herself. It was a pastel, princess cut affair that wouldn't go with her skin tone and wouldn't flatter her figure.

"Rusty, what's going on?"

"Don't ask any questions. Just put it on."

Ronnie flinched at his tone.

Rusty cursed under his breath, jerking his hand back. But then his resolve seemed to steel, and he held the dress out to her.

"I don't understand what's happening here?" Ronnie said. "Is this because of our argument the other day?"

"You know what," he said, clenching the gown in his fist. "You talk too much."

Rusty dropped the gown to the floor. He turned to the table, pulling his forearm to his torso as though he was about to swipe the food off the table.

"Rusty, no." Ronnie grabbed his forearm before he could take his anger out on the savory-smelling guacamole.

She had no idea what had gotten into him? He rarely displayed any anger. What was going on here?

She didn't have the chance to ask him. Rusty gripped her forearm and swung her into his chest. His powerful chest. It had been a long time since she'd been in this space.

Rusty's hand slipped down to the small of her back. That sense of relief flooded through Ronnie. She felt her soul rooting into the ground.

No. Her soul was rooting into this man.

No. Not rooting. She felt she was reconnecting into the soul where she had once flourished.

Rusty's lips took hers in a claiming kiss. His mouth crashed into hers, brooking no argument.

Allowing no room for escape. It was more forceful than any kiss they had ever shared.

At first, Ronnie pressed against his chest. This was so unlike him. He'd always been gentle with her. Passionate, yes. But never unyielding.

Instead of letting her go or loosening his grip, Rusty's hold tightened around her. A low growl escaped his mouth. It sent a shudder of desire through her. Any resistance went out of her.

Ronnie couldn't remember why they hadn't been doing this since the first day she'd gotten here. Oh wait, they had kissed that first day. When he'd fallen at his first sight of her. Then he'd opened his eyes, called her an angel, and took her lips.

Rusty had been back from overseas for months. They'd wasted all that time apart when they could've been together and kissing. Ronnie pulled him to her now, deepening the kiss.

She couldn't remember why she'd insisted on their separation? Something or other to do with romance? Who needed romance when they had this much chemistry between them?

But no. Chemistry wasn't the issue. When the kiss broke, when the day changed to night, the problems would still exist. What problems were those again?

The problem was that he always left. There was always another mission, an upcoming deployment, and he'd leave. He'd come home. It would be like a honeymoon all over again. They'd fall back into the routines, and at some point, he'd leave again. He always left.

"Russ, please," she said against his lips.

Rusty pulled back from her, but he didn't let her go. His gaze searched hers, eyes screwed in confusion. "This isn't what you want?"

Ronnie opened her mouth to say she didn't want this. That she didn't want him. But it was a lie.

She wanted him. She just didn't know how to have him. How to keep him. Because he would leave again.

"I followed everything to a T, Veronica."

"Followed? Followed what?"

Rusty rested his forehead against hers. "Ryker made Vanessa dinner and bought her a dress."

Ryker? Vanessa? Where had Rusty heard those names?

"He kissed her even when she said she didn't want him to. But in her head, she did."

"How would you know that? Have you been reading my book?"

"Yes, I read it." Rusty still hadn't let her go. He

was gripping her shoulders now. "It was the only way I could figure out what you wanted."

Ronnie pulled out of his hold and glared at him. "How could you? That was private?"

"Private? You put our lives on the page. You were about to share it with the rest of the world."

"*Seduced by the Sergeant* is not about us."

"Oh, yes, it is. But in the book, you gave me a chance. You won't in real life. Why?"

Ronnie turned away from him. The spices in the salsa hit her nose and caused it to wrinkle. The peppers made her eyes water.

"Why, Ronnie?" Rusty demanded.

"Because you're captive on the page. Because there you won't leave me."

"Leave you? I've never left you."

Ronnie turned away. Those peppers were really hot and doing a number on her eyes. Her stomach was in knots, letting her know that it would not hold down any of this food.

Rusty reached out to her, but this time it was Ronnie who turned to leave. However, as she did, a large figure clad in black burst through the door.

"This is a break-in," he growled in a low voice. A low, familiar voice.

"Grizz?" said Ronnie. "What are you doing?"

Grizz pulled the dark mask from his face. He looked from Ronnie to Rusty. "Sorry, man. I tried."

Ronnie looked between the two men, then at the dinner, and then the dress on the floor. Rusty had just manufactured a romantic evening, complete with a villain breaking in to interrupt an intimate moment.

Had it been on the page, it would've worked. But as this was her real life, the grand gesture fell completely flat.

CHAPTER FIFTEEN

*R*usty slept badly after last night's debacle of a romantic date. When the sun's rays touched his cheek, and he could no longer lay in bed, he rose. When he looked out the window, he felt he'd been tricked. Rain fell in heavy drops as the sun shone brightly.

He hated days like this. They were a contradiction. A rainstorm on a cloudless sky. That was much like his life these days. The skies were clear one moment, and then a storm came from out of nowhere in the next.

As he made his way down the hall, he saw that Ronnie's door was closed. There wasn't a single sound of stirring from within. He didn't knock. He wouldn't know what to say.

He'd fought hard for her over the last year during their separation. He'd caved and given her what she'd told him she wanted when he'd signed those missing divorce papers. He'd thrown caution to the wind when he'd acted out what he thought she wanted but left unsaid.

None of it had worked.

Rusty left the copy of her book on the dining room table. The table was cleared of all the dishes he'd had prepared for her. They were covered in foil or enclosed in Tupperware in the fridge.

Ronnie must have done that sometime after he'd stormed off last night. She didn't like to leave a mess. She couldn't sleep if dishes were left in the sink.

In fact, the entire place was orderly. The floors were swept. The appliances shone spotless. There were the pair of running shoes he'd misplaced a week ago lined up next to the door.

Rusty bent down and ran his hands over the lip of the shoes. She'd even tucked the strings inside. He couldn't help but smile.

Despite the fact that the woman drove him mad sometimes, he couldn't imagine his life without her. He knew she wanted to be with him. That had been desire in her gaze when she'd looked up at him. Before the surrender, serenity had settled on her features when she was in his arms. When his lips met hers, he'd felt his entire being latch into place, like a lock that had been missing the catch and finally fell back in place.

But then she'd pulled away.

Ronnie had said he was the one to leave, but she was always with him no matter where he was in this world. His every action was to secure her future. She was the one who'd thrown it all away. And for what?

"Found this," said Keaton when Rusty made his way to the training camp.

Keaton deposited a muddied cell phone in his hand. Rusty hadn't thought about his phone since he'd had Ronnie in the bedroom beside him for the past few days. The phone had been his only connection to her for the last year. It was useless now, having been left to the elements for days.

"So, the romance thing didn't work for you?" said Keaton.

Rusty shook his head. His chin lowered to his chest. He was glad he was looking down. His head was spinning, and there was a dull ache in his heart. He shouldn't have come to work today. He couldn't negotiate his own body into working correctly. He'd be of no use to anyone.

"I'm surprised," said Keaton. "It worked wonders for me and Brenda last night."

If the grin on the man's face wasn't clue enough, the wiggle of his eyebrows told Keaton had had a very enjoyable evening with his wife last night.

"I wore my uniform for Romey," said Spinelli. "She practically ripped it off me. Then later asked me to put it on again."

Rusty wanted to be happy for his friends. Just a year ago, when his marriage was falling apart, both of these men had sworn marriage was the farthest thing from their minds. Now, here they both were, happily married and having romantic evenings with their wives at his expense.

"What's this I'm hearing about romance novels?" said Mac, coming up to join their group. Grizz and Porco were a step behind him.

"Ronnie wrote one," said Grizz, scratching at the dark whiskers on his chin.

"Ronnie writes smut?" said Porco, popping a strip of fried bacon in his mouth.

"It's not smut," said Rusty.

"It's actually not," Grizz agreed. "It's the story of two people who you wouldn't expect to be together. Against all odds, they find each other and work through their problems to be together."

The way Grizz phrased it, the book sounded like a fairytale. Like make-believe.

"And there's bedroom stuff?" said Porco, popping another strip of bacon in his mouth.

"It's not about that," said Keaton. "It's about how they first work against each other and then work together to achieve their happy ending."

"I felt it was more of a woman's journey of self-discovery where she learns to believe in herself first and then open herself to love," said Grizz.

"Really?" said Spinelli. "I felt it was more of a treatise on the human condition."

The final piece of bacon was held before Porco's open mouth. He didn't slide it in his pie hole. Instead, he gaped at each of the men standing around him in utter disbelief and confusion.

"And yeah," said Keaton, "there's bedroom stuff. Man, I learned a few things."

"Hey." Rusty reached over and punched his friend in the chest. "That's my wife you're talking about."

"It's actually your wife's character," said Spinelli. "Which is why I don't understand why that scene last night didn't work. You played on all of her inner desires."

"The problem is, I don't think Ronnie knows what she wants," said Rusty.

"Do you know why you want her?" asked Spinelli.

Rusty frowned at the question. Then he opened his mouth to state the obvious, only to find that it wasn't so obvious. Why was he going through all this trouble to try and keep someone who wanted to run away from him? Why had he caught her in the first place?

He remembered the first time he'd seen her. Her smile had knocked him back. But it wasn't just her looks.

They'd talked for hours that first night. Well, she had done most of the talking. He'd listened. He loved listening to her. But had he fallen in love with her because he wanted a storyteller?

When he was near her, it just felt right. She felt like home to him. She set his world right. Not just with how she ran their household. He happily put his life in her hands and let her arrange it, so long as he got to care for her. He wanted to give her the world, but since that was too big, he'd given her his heart.

And she had handed it back to him.

"You're not going to give up," said Keaton. "Are you?"

The spinning sensation came back to him. So much so that Rusty couldn't even lift his head to look his friends in the eyes. He'd tried everything. He had nothing left to give because there was nothing the love of his life wanted from him.

CHAPTER SIXTEEN

*R*onnie gathered her research notes into one arm. She tucked her laptop in the other and went out onto the deck of the bungalow. The sun had dried the droplets from the freak rainstorm from the morning. She loved it when it rained on a sunny day. The contradiction delighted her.

She'd stayed up late last night to put away the dishes Rusty had laid out on the table. Her stomach had been tied in such tight knots that she couldn't eat a bite. Now she brought the food out onto the deck, but she still couldn't bring herself to eat a single bite.

She couldn't believe the length he'd gone to last night. Flattery and anger were still warring in her head. Rusty had never done anything like that before. Likely because he'd never known that it was her fantasy.

What was it that Mrs. Patel had said? She had to take her husband out on dates to show him what she wanted. But shouldn't he just know?

Ronnie supposed not. Even though Rusty had read the details of her dream date, he'd still gotten it wrong.

She pushed last night out of her mind. She had too much work to do. Work that would ensure her future; a future that didn't include Rusty.

She set her research notebooks, model photographs, and miscellaneous paperwork aside. Tapping the keys to open her Word document, Ronnie read through her manuscript.

The end still wasn't sitting well with her. Ryker and Vanessa had been through every obstacle she as an author had thrown at them. Forces had tried to keep them apart, but they always found their way back to one another time and time again.

She was nearing the end of the story. This was the climax. This was the last challenge they would face. But something was off.

For this final climax, Ronnie couldn't find a way to get her hero and heroine back together.

Everything she tried read as forced and unplausible. The ending was playing out more like a tragedy than a romance.

Ronnie closed the Word file and pulled up an Excel spreadsheet. She needed to give the creative side of her brain a rest. So she decided to do some administrative work instead. In the rows and columns of the spreadsheet were names and fees for book editors. The problem was that Ronnie wasn't sure which type of editor to choose.

There was a list of developmental editors who would go over the structure of her book and tell her whether it was good or not. But what if they didn't like her story? What if their suggestions would lead to a rewrite of her work?

Then there were the line editors. Their job was to look closely at her sentence structure. Ronnie hadn't paid the best attention in English class. She'd preferred to read the assigned books rather than fuss over the grammar and repetition of words. What did it matter how many times you used a word if it was the right word for the scene?

It didn't stop after the line editor. There were also copy editors and proofreaders. Then beta readers and ARC readers. It was overwhelming. And would eat into most of her funds. Not to mention that most of the editors she'd contacted were booked up for months in advance. Which meant she wouldn't be turning a profit anytime soon. No profit meant no money for rent and necessities.

She didn't want to go back to her parents. Though all of her siblings had homes of their own, her parents' house was grandparents central. There were always people over. Ronnie would get even less peace there than when she was a child.

All she wanted was a quiet place where she could get her work done. She could stay here with Rusty. Not that he'd want her here any longer after last night's argument.

That had been their worst fight ever. In the past, when they'd disagreed, Rusty would listen quietly, trying to patiently and logically negotiate with her. Last night he'd been emotional. His final words to her had been filled with anger. And all that after he'd tried to give her the romance she said she wanted.

But what he'd done hadn't been real. It had been from the pages of a book. Her book. He'd tried to give her what she wanted only to find out it wasn't what she wanted from him.

She didn't like Rusty manhandling her, where he'd always been gentle but passionate. She didn't like him bossing her around, where he'd always talked things through with her.

So what did she want from him?

Ronnie scratched at the hollow spot at her low back. She remembered when he'd pulled her to him. He'd settled his hand there, and she'd felt that sense of security. He'd pressed his lips to hers, and she'd felt light like nothing could touch her. But now she was left insecure and weighed down with indecision.

"Hi, Ronnie."

Ronnie looked up to see Patty waddling toward her. The woman's belly wasn't protruding, but her pregnancy was getting more and more noticeable. Patty wasn't alone. Lana was with her. Along with Keaton's wife and the two twins who were married to Porco and Spinelli. They had platters in their hands.

"We brought lunch," said one of the twins. She was the one with the longer hair; Jules was her name. Jules put a plate of squishy white blocks before Ronnie. Ronnie leaned back in her chair at the unfamiliar fare.

"And sandwiches," said Brenda, putting down ham and cheese sandwiches in front of the edible sponges.

"To each his own," Jules muttered as she plopped a squishy blob in her mouth.

"We came for gossip," said Lana, taking a seat beside Ronnie. "We heard what happened last night."

Ronnie groaned. Partly because she didn't want to rehash what had happened last night. But also because she didn't want a back porch full of women who she'd have to leave in a few days.

"Did Rusty really get decked out in his uniform?" Lana asked.

Ronnie nodded as she closed her laptop. The smell of ham had her reaching out for a sandwich. She flipped over a slice of bread and smeared guacamole on it.

"I thought it was sweet," said Patty. "They tried to recreate your book for you. Your book was fabulous, by the way."

"You read my book?" said Ronnie around a mouthful of savory ham.

"To help Grizz get into character," said Patty after taking a bite of her own sandwich. "Thank you for not stabbing him, by the way."

"You're welcome," Ronnie mumbled, her mind still on the fact that others had read her book. She wondered if everyone on this ranch had passed around the copy. She wanted to let them know it wasn't the final version.

"I didn't read it," said Romey, the twin with the shorter, springy curls. "But Jordan recounted it for us. He has a photographic memory."

Beside her, her sister Jules looked skyward, fluttering her lashes. "I loved the part where Ryker finally drops to his knees and admits he can't live without Vanessa."

"That's because you're a hopeless romantic," said her twin.

"Guilty," said Jules, plopping another spongey blob into her mouth.

"There were a few grammar errors," said Lana, her tone delicate. "I could help you with those if you like. I worked at a magazine for years."

That's right, Lana was a writer. The two had had a great conversation about Jane Austen's heroes years ago. Captain Wentworth was Ronnie's favorite while Mr. Tilney was Lana's. Mr. Darcy didn't rank in the top five for either woman.

"We could also get Sarai Cannon to take a look, too," Lana went on. "She's another writer. She lives next door on the Purple Heart Ranch."

"What are you going to do about the cover?" said Patty, her voice wasn't as delicate as Lana's. Patty had always been a straight-forward kinda girl. "I think it should be a bare-chested man. You can use my husband if you want."

"I don't know, Patty," said Brenda. "Grizz is putting on pregnancy weight alongside you."

Patty threw a bread crumb at Brenda. The tall ranch woman ducked the missive with ease. They all were laughing at the antics. Like old friends.

Ronnie sat in the circle of laughter. It washed over her like an unstoppable wave. Because Ronnie couldn't stop this from happening. She liked these women.

"Since last night didn't go well, are you and Rusty still getting a divorce?" That came from Romey, Spinelli's wife. It was clear the two were meant to be. She was just as direct as her husband.

"Are you already dating someone else?"

Ronnie was looking down. She didn't know the women well enough by voice to know who'd asked that. The thought of dating anyone else had never occurred to her. The women must have seen the revulsion on her face at the idea.

"Do you still love him?"

Ronnie didn't lift her gaze. Her lips pursed as she fought to keep hold of the answer. But she was sure the women saw her chest beating an answer against her tank top.

"Why not try to make it work? Rusty is such a good guy."

Rusty was the best guy. But when he left, when he turned to his work over her, it hurt more than she could bear. One night of candles and pretty words weren't enough to smooth that over.

And that's when she knew that romance wasn't what she wanted. What she had always wanted—what she had only wanted—was his presence. For him to stay with her and never leave. For him to not put himself in danger to give her the life he thought she wanted.

She knew that was selfish. She could never speak those words aloud on a base. But she wasn't on a base any longer. She was on a ranch.

And so she looked up. She opened her mouth to speak what was truly in her heart. And there he was.

CHAPTER SEVENTEEN

*R*usty had no idea what to expect when he came back home that afternoon. It certainly wasn't the entire community of women gathered in his back yard. He could barely handle the one he wanted to gather into his arms.

Ronnie rose to greet him. "Hey."

"Hey," said Rusty, standing in the back door. He felt as though there was a boundary line between the inside of the house and the outside. The distance was short to Ronnie, but he was certain the ground between them was laid with land mines.

"You're home early," Ronnie said, biting her lower lip.

Rusty's gaze tracked the movement. His hands itched to bring her to him. His mouth watered to taste the spot where she'd bitten. But even more, his heart pounded at the words she'd said to him.

There was something so domestic about the way she'd said that word; *home*.

Rusty had come home. In a place they shared together. He'd come back sooner than he'd planned. He couldn't help himself. Whenever he returned from a mission or a deployment, he spent his every waking hour with her, unsure how long his stay would last.

Sure, he left. It was part of his job. But couldn't she see that his every move was always to get back to her? He wanted nothing more than to hold her in his arms for the rest of his days.

Ronnie's arms were crossed over her chest. She hugged herself, providing the comfort he wanted to give. She didn't want his comfort because she thought it was transitory.

"I didn't mean to interrupt." Rusty motioned to the women seated in chairs.

None of them made to move. The other wives watched him and Ronnie as though they were a live-action soap opera.

"I can leave." The words grated as they passed Rusty's lips.

His heart had taken up permanent residence in

Ronnie's soul. Yet she was trying to evict him. It was a doomed mission. Because he wasn't going to leave. It was impossible. She was a part of him, and he was never giving that back.

"No!" Ronnie took a step toward him, her hand stretched out to him.

Rusty's first instinct was to gather his wife up in his arms and pull her to him. But those instincts had failed him last night. So he shut his mouth, and he held his place.

They stood before each other. The silence should have been awkward, but it was familiar. He stared into Ronnie's eyes, searching for something.

And then he found it.

Something had changed there. It wasn't something new. It was something old. There was an openness he hadn't seen in a long time. In that opening was a light. Just a small glimmer. But he recognized it.

It was hope.

Rusty's heart had been beating sluggishly all morning. Now it kicked into gear. His mind raced with negotiation protocol. Contain her. Isolate her. Skip talking negotiations and make her surrender with seduction.

"They brought the welcome wagon," said

Ronnie, gesturing behind her to the women around the table.

Rusty lifted his gaze to look over Ronnie's head. The women were all leaning in. Rusty narrowed his eyes to slits as he looked at each woman in turn. His intention was to communicate to them all to get lost.

Not a single one of them moved.

It wasn't that his threatening glare was out of practice. He'd stared down insurgents only months ago. He dealt with the ire of wanna-be Rangers crawling through the mud and obstacle courses of the training camp each week. He managed Keaton on a daily basis.

But so did each of these women. One of his friends' wives on her own, he might be able to scare off with a look. All of them?

"Ladies, our husbands will be arriving home soon," said Brenda. "We should probably get these leftovers to them so they can have an appetizer before dinner."

The other four women didn't move a muscle at Brenda's subtle command.

"Up!" Brenda snapped her fingers, which worked to kick the women in gear. Keaton would be so proud.

Their movements were slow and grudging,

especially Patty's. Though Rusty had seen her move quickly the other day when Grizz chased her through one of the fields. Soon, but not soon enough, they all started back up the path to the main house.

"I thought you weren't keen on making new friends," Rusty said once he and Ronnie were alone.

"They didn't give me a choice."

She was contained and isolated. But he had no idea how to get her to surrender. He ached to simply take her in his arms, but he'd learned his lesson.

"Ronnie, I'm sorry about last night."

"I know."

"I thought that was what you wanted; for me to take charge like that and not give you a choice."

"Me, too," she said, shaking her head as though clearing fog. "But it's just a fantasy. It doesn't work in real life."

"What do you want in real life?"

She looked up at him. Her eyes were clear. The spark of hope Rusty had seen a moment ago reached the edges of her pupils.

Was it enough? He wasn't sure. So he held his ground, but he spoke his truth.

"I love you," Rusty said with a shrug.

"Yeah, I know." Ronnie mirrored his shrug. "I love you, too."

"So, why are we..." Rusty motioned at the distance between them. "Why isn't that enough for you?"

"Because you make me feel like a balloon."

"I...what?"

"Every time you come around, I get inflated. You puff a little more into me each time. Then when you leave, I deflate until it feels like there's nothing left of me. Then you come back, and the process begins over again until I'm left sagging and formless."

Her hands motioned up and down her lush curves. A deflated balloon is the last thing Rusty would compare Ronnie to. But he doubted complimenting her body was the right tactic at the moment.

"I forgot who I was." She looked down at her hands as though they didn't belong to her. Then she turned to her open laptop on the table. "I think that's why the book isn't working. I'm confused about what love looks like."

Ronnie turned back to him. The hope in her eyes had dimmed and only despair showed through. Rusty wanted to tell her that love looked like a man willing to do anything to make a woman smile. Love was fighting so hard you couldn't see straight.

"At least I *was* confused about what love is," she said. "Then you fixed my car. And you co-signed my dream. And you made a complete fool of yourself last night."

Yeah, and it looked like that, too.

Ronnie closed the distance between them. Rusty's arms reached out to contain her. He pulled her into his body to isolate them from the rest of the world. His hands negotiated the curve of her spine until they came to rest at her low back. Ronnie's sigh was pure surrender as she closed her eyes and rested her head against his chest.

"This is what love feels like," she said.

Rusty wasn't sure what she meant. He wasn't even kissing her yet. He didn't feel the need. He had her close. That was all he wanted, to keep her close and safe in his arms. And so he did.

Rusty wrapped Ronnie up in his arms, and he held onto her. Tightening his hold with every minute that passed. She didn't offer a single mumble of protest.

"Russell?"

"Yes, Veronica?"

"I want to negotiate terms."

"Terms for what?"

"Reconciliation."

Rusty pulled her even tighter. If she were the sagging balloon she complained of, she would've burst. But he'd put the pieces of her back together.

The sun peeked from behind a cloud. As it did, a light rain started to sprinkle as the rays shone down. For once, Rusty didn't mind the contradiction. All the grit and grime of the past year washed away from his hard exterior to leave behind a bright afterglow of happiness.

Ronnie, however, jumped in his arms. Rusty tightened his grip. He'd let her go once. That was never happening again.

"I have to get my things from the table," she protested

It took Rusty a couple of strides to get to the table and swipe everything up in his arms. Ronnie relieved him of her laptop, tucking it under her shirt for protection, lucky piece of technology. When he got inside, he looked down at the documents in his hands.

Notebooks that looked well worn. Spreadsheets with names and figures. Photographs of shirtless men. Rusty looked past the shirtless men and his gaze rested on a familiar envelope.

"Oh, that's yours. Pastor Vance brought it by a couple of days ago. I'm so sorry. I completely forgot to give it to you."

Rusty's fingers trembled as he held the missive. Unfortunately, he was holding it upside down, and the documents slipped out. Ronnie sat the laptop on the kitchen table and bent to pick up the documents. Her face fell when she realized what she held.

"These are the divorce papers," she said.

Rusty said nothing.

"You signed them?"

CHAPTER EIGHTEEN

The documents trembled in her fingers.

The pages fluttering like wings upset by a sudden wind. Ronnie held tight lest they get away from her.

She glanced at her signature on the document. The V in her name looked like a checkmark. A tick in the box in her bid to dissolve the union between her and Rusty.

Although the V had almost become a W. Her hands had shaken as she'd put the pen to paper. She'd nearly asked for a new signature page. She'd been sure Rusty had seen her hesitancy in her scrawl. She'd been sure that that's what had kept him from placing his signature beside hers.

There had always been some part of her that

never expected to see this. But there it was, in black and white. There was no wiggle in Rusty's signature. The pen marks were straight and sure.

Their marriage was over. Just after the very second when she thought it was saved.

Ronnie released her hold on the document. The pages fluttered to the floor, landing in a resounding thud. She wrapped her arms around herself. She felt as though she was going to float away. Why hadn't she thought that this was the conclusion of her actions?

She wanted to take the papers and rip them up. She wanted to burn them out of existence. The sound of a tear brought her mind back to the present. Rusty's powerful hands were rending the document into two. Then he took the two halves, and for good measure, he tore those bits to shreds as well.

"It doesn't make a difference," he said. "It never had, not even when I signed it."

Ronnie could only stare at his hands. Those powerful hands that could rip a stack of papers, but could also make her feel grounded and safe. Those hands came up to her face and cupped her chin.

"I gave you my vow," Rusty continued. "No inkblot can ever take that away."

"You signed." Even as she said the words, she recognized they had no weight. The only weight she felt was Rusty's hand slowly moving down to anchor at her back.

"I did," he nodded. "I thought I had no more cards to play, so I gave in to your demands."

"I was wrong."

"Yeah, I know."

A strangled laugh escaped Ronnie's throat. A soft chuckle left Rusty's lips. He rested his forehead against hers.

"Russ?"

"Yeah, Ron?"

"I know what I want now."

"Tell me."

"I want to be with you."

A slow grin spread across Rusty's handsome face. He lifted his head from hers. In doing so, his lips brushed lightly across hers.

"No, not physically." Ronnie shook her head. "I mean, yes, physically. But I want more than that. You stopped talking to me when you came home from overseas."

"I did?" There was confusion in those two words.

"You closed yourself off to me. And I understand some part of why. You saw awful things overseas, and you wanted to protect me from it. But I lost a part of you when you shut me out. I don't want to be shut out anymore."

Rusty didn't immediately respond. He didn't let her go either. He held her in his arms as he turned her words over in his mind.

"You're right," he said finally. "I didn't want any ugliness to touch you from my work. I did everything in my power to make the world safer for you. If I could, I'd have built a wall around you to make sure the bad guys never got close to you."

"I don't want to be locked away unless you're with me."

"I can arrange that," Rusty grinned. "We could live here."

"In the bungalow?"

"No. Here on the ranch. We each got an acre of land as part of the deal we signed. Mac, Grizz, and I are going to build houses. I'll build your dream house. We can go out later, and you can choose a reading tree."

Ronnie's eyes lit up at that thought. Plus, a home where she got to put down roots. Friends that she never had to say goodbye to. And Rusty working just a few miles down the road and home every night.

"Yes," she said. "Under one condition."

"Name it."

"Little Patty Keaton is pregnant," she said.

"She's Patty Hayes now."

"I want to be pregnant, too."

Rusty swallowed. His gaze did a slow scan of her body. Before his eyes came back to her face, he said, "Let's get started."

Ronnie found herself being swept off her feet then. She grinned into Rusty's lips as he pressed his claim. She gave herself over to his command, ready to yield to his every directive.

The chiming of a cell phone interrupted the mood of the moment. As if to punctuate the intrusion, Ronnie felt a buzzing against her thigh, which was pressed against Rusty's pant leg as he held her up.

"I thought this thing was dead." Rusty shifted his hold of her to one arm and reached in his pocket for his phone with the other. "Let me just..."

He looked at the screen and his features pinched. Ronnie knew that look. It was the look he got whenever he was being called in to be spun up for a mission.

"It's okay," said Ronnie, wiggling to get out of his hold.

Rusty set her down as he thumbed a button on

the device, but he didn't let her go. "Dr. Patel? What is it?"

Rusty's voice wasn't curt, even though their amorous activity had just been interrupted. Rusty sounded genuinely concerned. Ronnie couldn't hear the other part of the conversation. But she watched Rusty's expression turn grim.

He winced when he looked back at her, his expression turning pained. Ronnie knew that look too. Their amorous activities were about to be postponed.

"I'll be there as soon as I can." Rusty clicked off and turned to her. "I'm sorry, Ronnie, but one of the vets has gone missing. He's had some psychological problems. They asked if I can help find him."

"I understand." And she did. Her raging hormones could take a backseat while her husband went to save someone's life. Especially since he'd given her a brief of his mission. And also because it wouldn't take him overseas, just down the road.

"I'll be back soon," he said.

"I'll be here," she said.

"I love you."

For the last year, those words had weighed heavily on Ronnie's heart whenever he said them to her. Today, they made her feel like she could fly. "I love you."

Rusty pressed his lips to hers. A soft gentle kiss that was heavy with promise. He grinned at her as he pulled away. "I have you back."

It was a whisper. She wasn't sure if it was for him or for her, but she held onto those words. He did have her back. And she had him back. She would have him with her for the rest of her days.

CHAPTER NINETEEN

For almost a year, Rusty had wracked his brain for the words that would convince his wife to give their marriage a second chance. He'd scoured old textbooks and documents on negotiation strategies and tactics to use to his advantage. In the end, the thing that had worked had been giving Ronnie what she thought she wanted, only to see that it was the last thing she cared to have.

Which was funny, when he thought of it. Rusty had fought the inevitable for months. And the moment he let go, she came back to him. He'd had Ronnie back in his arms. He'd kissed her senseless, and she'd given in to his desires.

He had no idea how he'd just walked away from

that dream come true and out the door. Especially when his being called away at a moment's notice, and his long absences had contributed to the downfall of his marriage. That edict of military life was a difficult one when a man had a family. The balance was near impossible. But this time, when duty called, it wouldn't pull him too far for too long.

The Purple Heart Ranch had a brother missing. The soldier needed his help. The United States Military never left one of their own behind. Not even when they were on home soil.

"Private Reggie Williams was last seen at 0800 this morning," said Dylan. "We became aware that something was amiss when Private Williams missed his check-in at the clinic."

Rusty looked down at the photograph of the man. In the picture, Private Williams stared straight ahead, no smile on his face as was the way in a military photograph. This was the man Dr. Patel and Dylan had asked him to lend a hand with the day Ronnie got here.

Private Williams looked like every fresh-faced soldier. There was that light in his eye that he was eager to serve his country. Along with the lift to his chin that he wanted to be cast in the role of hero.

They all did. They all were. But war clipped many men and women's capes.

"I feel obliged to share with you the Reggie was experiencing post-traumatic episodes over our last few sessions," said Dr. Patel. "He was having trouble keeping his grip on the present moment."

The collective sigh that went through the room of soldiers was silent. It was the heaviness in the air that touched Rusty's ears. Each man had their own demons that they battled with after leaving the service. Some were external scars. But most were hidden deep in their chests.

"So, he thinks he's back on the battlefield?" asked Keaton.

"No," said Dr. Patel. "Private Williams wasn't flashing back to combat. He's been reliving his conflicts with the red tape of the government."

Dr. Patel explained how Reggie Williams had been denied some of his benefits. The type of injury Reggie experienced, a traumatic brain injury or TBI, was still a new diagnosis in the military. TBIs left many a soldier disabled after their time in service. However, because they were rarely diagnosed during combat, because it could put the brakes on their career, many soldiers left the service with the injury in tow and no records of its initial appearance. This made claiming a TBI as a disability after separation a daunting task.

"Private Williams feels that if he had the disability and the added benefits it came with, then he could've afforded to buy his wife a home and she wouldn't have left him."

Rusty scratched at his chest. The man's story was tragic. A few more knocks to the head, and it could've been the unhappy ending for anyone gathered in the room. There was a resolve on each man's face to find their injured brother.

"We've called you all in here to help with the search because..." Dylan took a deep breath before continuing. "It appears someone has broken into the weapons locker."

The stance of each man in the room changed in a split second. The level of danger raised up to the roof. Each man had a family on this land that he was willing to lay down his life for.

"You're saying we have an armed man, who is trained in combat, and experiencing episodes in bureaucratic conflict?" Rusty ticked each issue off with his fingers.

"That's the right of it," said Dylan, his expression grave.

"You think he's gone back to his wife?" asked Keaton.

"She's clear across the country," said Dylan. "And she has a protective order against him. I think he's likely gone to the VA in Fort Harris to confront them over his financial woes."

It was that phrasing that sparked Rusty's memories. His mind flashed back to just a couple of days ago. The man he'd seen inside the bank. That man had not been the clean-shaven soldier in the picture. He'd looked like a homeless man. But it was the eyes that connected the dots.

"I think I know where he is," said Rusty.

CHAPTER TWENTY

*R*onnie pulled up to the bank. Unlike the first day here, her car didn't screech when she pressed the brakes to stop. Bessie was riding like a car ten years younger thanks to Rusty. Ronnie patted the steering wheel before she stepped out of the driver's side door.

Taking the uncashed bank check out of her purse, she headed to the glass doors. She no longer needed the bank's money. Perhaps this was why she hadn't cashed it. Perhaps she'd known there wouldn't be a need for it.

She had two editors lined up to clean up her words in Lana and Sarai. She'd settled on Porco as her male model, much to the ire of the other men. And she'd also learned that another wife on the

Purple Heart Ranch was good with marketing. She'd need to spend a fraction of the money to bring her book to the world.

And that fraction would come from the joint bank account she shared with her husband. This book was as much his tale as it was hers. Just as his service had been just as much hers.

To top off finally claiming her authorial dreams, she was also getting her dream home. Ronnie didn't care about the specs of the place. The only requirement she had of her dream home was that her dream man live in it with her.

Rusty would be there for her. Not just physically. He'd pledged to be there for her emotionally as well. And, she hoped, there would be more romance tossed in. She could even do with being swept off her feet and manhandled every now and again. So long as her husband was the man to do it.

The divorce papers were in the trash bin where they belonged. Rusty wasn't gone. He wasn't deployed. He was just a couple miles down the road looking for a missing soldier.

He was coming back. To her. To their home.

This could be their home, a place with roots to plant themselves forever. They could finally start a family together. Oh boy, did she want to get to work on that endeavor. But first thing's first.

Ronnie clutched the check in hand and headed into the bank. She sought out the chauvinist banker, but he wasn't at his desk. Mr. Denton was standing with a customer. But the haughty sneer wasn't on his face today.

His features were a mismatched hodgepodge. His eyes were large, open so wide they nearly touched his hairline. His lips were rounded in a small, pinched O. His cheeks were flushed red. He was sweating from his brow and shaking from his shoulders down. Put all together it looked like fear.

Ronnie knew she'd guessed Mr. Denton's mood right when his gaze darted to her in the doorway. His gaze narrowed, as though imploring her to help him. That was a weird turn of events. What could she possibly do to help him? Other than give him back the check she no longer needed.

Ronnie held up the check as though to indicate to Mr. Denton that that's what she'd come to do. That's when the customer standing in front of Mr. Denton turned around.

Ronnie recognized him instantly. He was the scruffy looking man who had been in the bank the day she'd gotten her loan. That man had walked out of the doors empty-handed. His hands weren't empty any longer.

"Don't scream," the man said, waving the gun at her. "Don't run, and no one will get hurt."

"Okay," Ronnie said soothingly.

Her back was against the closed glass door. She knew she couldn't reach behind her and yank it open faster than a bullet could catch her. She also knew that calm was the best defense in these matters. Rusty had taught her that.

Rusty? She wished he was here with her now. He would know how to handle this situation. He'd talked men out of suicide vests and down from high ledges. What would Rusty do in this situation?

Contain. Isolate. Negotiate.

They were all contained in the four walls of the bank. There were five of them in isolation. Ronnie, the gunman, Mr. Denton, and the two tellers. Luckily, there were no other civilians inside. Now it was time to negotiate.

"Maybe I can help?" said Ronnie, taking a step closer to them. "You need money? That's why you're in the bank. How much do you need?"

The gunman's gaze flicked to the check-in her hand. "I don't want your money. I wouldn't take money from a woman."

That's when she saw it. This man may look disheveled, but his shoulders were erect. His head was high. His posture perfect. Only one type of man had that countenance in him at all times.

"You're a soldier, aren't you?"

The gunman didn't answer. He turned the gun back on the bank manager. "I just want what they owe me."

"We don't owe you anything," said Mr. Denton. "We're not the U.S. government or the VA. You need to take your issue there."

The sound of the safety flicking off brought whimpers around the bank. Mr. Denton shut his eyes. Tears streamed down his cheeks.

"I was right." Ronnie took a step closer, still keeping her hands up. "You are a soldier. You having some trouble with your VA paperwork?"

He didn't look at Ronnie. But his jaw tensed, letting her know she'd struck a nerve.

"I know what it's like to deal with all that red tape and paperwork," she said, trying to keep her tone friendly. "I've got permanent paper cuts to prove it. I'm a military wife. My husband is Sgt. Russell Hook. Do you know him?"

The gunman's jaw relaxed, but he didn't speak.

"What's your name, soldier?"

It took forever, but he answered. "Private Reggie Williams, ma'am."

This was good. If he gave his name he was less likely to hurt them. He'd also called her *ma'am*, which meant his manners were still intact. Polite people didn't usually go about shooting others.

"I can help you with the paperwork. I've gotten pretty good at it. What do you say we get on the phone and talk with someone from the VA?"

Reggie turned to face her. They were only a few footsteps away from each other now. His hand began to lower as his gaze rose to her face. But when the front door of the bank slammed open, Reggie's gaze flicked away from her, and his hand raised.

"Get away from my wife."

Ronnie looked up to see Rusty. His broad shoulders darkened the doorway like an avenging angel. Ronnie's instinct was to go to him and fold herself into his chest. But she couldn't move. There was a hand around her neck and a gun pointed at her temple.

CHAPTER TWENTY-ONE

*R*usty's life had flashed before his eyes many times in the theater of battle. It was the same set of scenes each time an explosive had gone off too near him. Or a bullet whizzed past him. Or a hostile got a caged look in their eyes when the negotiations soured.

Each time the end looked like it was near, Rusty's mind would rewind and do a life review. He never saw a single scene of battle or his time of service in that split second. His family featured prominently, his mom and dad's faces taking a good twenty percent of that single tick of time.

His military brothers' faces flickered for a tenth of that second. The five men were all smiling and laughing. There was not a hint of remorse from a single one of them. They'd each known the cost of their service could add up to the ultimate sacrifice. They'd each gotten up each morning prepared to tender that bill if duty called.

Still, each of those memories, those of his family and his friends, were but a fleeting instant. The remaining balance of that split second accounting of Rusty's life was spent on Ronnie.

Ronnie with her head buried in a book. Ronnie with the light of laughter in her gaze. Ronnie with a flare of desire in her eyes.

Funny that not a single flash he saw of her showed any of the ire that had come between them in the last year. He supposed that time in their lives wasn't worth remembering. She looked at him now with absolute horror in her wide eyes.

Her face was ashen, a sickly white. Those lush curls radiated out from her crown, but a piece of steel held some of the curls back. The steel was a gun.

A man held a gun to Ronnie's temple.

Rusty's training should've kicked in. He should be trying to get the man to talk. He should remember that this was a fellow soldier who was in need of help. But all Rusty saw was red.

He'd been trained in all forms of hostage

negotiation, including what to do in terms of a bank robbery. He knew that the last place a negotiator wanted to be was inside the establishment. It would've been best to set up outside and out of sight. To call in and establish communication via phone.

Rusty's feet didn't budge from the doorway. He shut the door behind him so that no one else could come in. He'd contained the threat. They were all isolated together. All that was left to do was negotiate.

"Point it at me," Rusty said calmly.

Reggie Williams flinched. It was as though the man's brain had heard the command of a superior and was warring against disobeying a direct order. "I just want what they owe me."

"We're fine," said Ronnie. "Everything's fine. This is my friend, Reggie."

There was a tremor in Ronnie's voice. She'd gotten the man's name out of him. That was good. She must have remembered what Rusty had told her about hostage negotiations. The old adage for a hostage to make themselves familiar with their captive.

But, like the tremor in Ronnie's voice, as she introduced her new friend, there was also a tremor in Reggie's hand. The hand that held the gun to the head of the person Rusty held most dear in the world. That thrust the potential of Reggie's and Rusty's friendship down the drain.

"He's upset over his disability," Ronnie continued, her voice growing stronger. "I told him I could help him with the paperwork because I'm good at that."

"I just want what I'm owed," said Reggie, the tremor of uncertainty still in his voice.

"Private Williams, I'm going to need you to stop pointing the gun at my wife and train it on me."

"She's your wife?"

Reggie lowered the gun a fraction. Rusty's instinct was to charge the man and grab Ronnie. But there was still a chance the gun would go off in the kerfuffle, and she might be hurt. Too risky.

"My wife left me," said Reggie, lowering the gun another fraction.

"I left him, too," said Ronnie, turning slightly in the gunman's hold. "But I came back. We talked it out. Now we're back together, stronger than before."

Ronnie wasn't looking at him, but Rusty knew the words were meant for his ears. She was using her story time voice. The one Rusty could listen to for hours and be lulled into a peaceful respite. It was working on Reggie.

"I can't talk to my Janie," Reggie said. "She put a restraining order on me."

Rusty felt for the guy. He really did. But the gun was lowered to Reggie's side. Ronnie was out of danger.

Reggie was no longer looking up. He was looking off in the distance, thoughtful. Rusty could've used his words and negotiated a peaceful end to this scene.

Instead, he charged the man.

CHAPTER TWENTY-TWO

*W*hen Rusty had rushed past her, Ronnie's life had flashed before her eyes. The reel was all too brief. Images of her family flickered, much like an old cinema reel gaining speed.

Ronnie saw her mother frowning at the jewel-coated romance cover of *The Flame and the Flower* in her twelve-year-old hands. But instead of the scolding Ronnie had insisted she'd gotten, she now remembered that her mother had slipped her a worn copy of Judy Blume's *Forever...* Her mother had insisted that if she was going to read romance, it shouldn't be of men ripping a woman's bodice. It needed to be one that featured smart girls learning there was no shame in their bodies.

There was a flash of Ronnie's sister looking angry after Ronnie had snuck a book from her stash. But the annoyance of her memory died and was replaced with her sister handing her the first book in that series and recouped book four, with a promise to lend Ronnie that work after she'd caught up.

There was a glimmer of her English teacher's disapproving face as she looked over Ronnie's textbook to see a romance novel inside the pages. But instead of the chiding Ronnie recalled, she recollected that the woman had slipped her a copy of *Pride and Prejudice*, insisting that if Ronnie was going to read romance, then it needed to be quality literature.

After all of those retouched reflections, there was nothing but flashes of Rusty. Rusty's mouth tugging into a grin. Rusty's eyes lighting with desire. Rusty's hands pulling her close.

The sensation of safety, of security, flooded Ronnie as the reel of her life played on. But there was no end to the reel. The last image was not of his face. It was of his chest. Because that's what she saw now.

Ronnie was pressed into Rusty's chest, held close to his beating heart. His hand was at her lower back, giving her that sensation of being rooted. Because he was her home, her present, her future.

The images of him hit her so hard, so fast that Ronnie was breathless when she looked up and was treated to the reality of his handsome face. Her husband was there in the flesh. Whole and unharmed and holding her.

He wasn't grinning down at her. His gaze flared, but with anger. His hold on her was more painful than pleasurable.

"What are you doing here?" he shouted. "You could've..."

He didn't complete the sentence. Instead, he pulled her back to him. His hold was even firmer, a padded lock Ronnie doubted she would ever break. She knew she'd never want to.

"I came to return the check," she said as she rubbed her hands up and down her husband's back, trying to infuse the sense of safety and security she always felt when he did the same to her.

After long moments, Rusty gave. But it was less than an inch. As she had predicted, his hold on her didn't break as she squirmed to get a look at the aftermath.

Mr. Denton was seated in a chair, a handkerchief pressed to his forehead as he dotted away the sweat on his brow. And perhaps a few tears from his cheek. Tossing the check-in his face or ripping it up would be anticlimactic after having saved the man's life.

Reggie Williams was on the ground. He wasn't being held. Keaton and Dylan Banks stood over him. Reggie's head was in his hands, his body rocked with tremors, his face contorted in misery.

There was resignation in his light eyes. He'd given up. Despite what he'd just done, the crime he'd committed, and the danger he'd caused, Ronnie felt sorry for him.

"He needs help," she said.

Rusty sighed. The sound was weary, as though there was some give. But still, his hold on her remained absolute. "He'll get it. He has to face the wrong he's done here today. But then, after, help will be waiting for him at the Purple Heart Ranch. He's a brother. We don't leave our brothers behind. Even if we want to beat the crap out of them."

Rusty pulled her closer. Then Ronnie was airborne. He'd swept her off her feet and was whisking her away from the danger. He didn't set her down until they were outside the building.

The cool breeze of the day lifted the curls of her hair. Her bottom was cold as steel as Rusty sat her on the hood of Old Bessie. Once she was perched onto the car, he finally let her go.

Rusty took a step back from her, and a tremor went through his body. He looked as though he might swoon.

"Russ?"

"My work has never touched you before," he said. "You've never been in danger of being a hostage."

She wanted to tell him that that wasn't true. That she'd been a hostage as long as she'd known him. A willing one that had fallen for the man who'd captured her heart. But she doubted he'd care to hear such romantic overtures at the time.

"You're my world, Veronica."

Or maybe he had some overtures of his own he wanted to dish out. Ronnie was here for that.

"You took my heart hostage from the first moment I saw you. I knew that no matter what happened, I would forever be yours. I became your hostage, body, and soul."

Part of Ronnie wished she had a pen and paper to write this purple prose down. But she knew that each word Rusty uttered was being written on her heart.

"Whatever terms you want in order to stay," he continued, "name them, and they're yours."

Ronnie held her arms open. Rusty came inside them. He wrapped his arms around her, resting his hand in the place it belonged at the small of her back.

"What I want is to live with you happily ever after."

"Ever after, I can promise," he said. "Happily I might fall short of from time to time."

"It's okay. I've learned the value of having a good editor."

Rusty sighed as he pressed his lips to hers. Ronnie had kissed her husband before, thousands of times. But this kiss was different. It was more. It was the first chapter in the sequel to their life's story. And Ronnie knew that his new journey would be a sweeping, epic romance for the ages.

EPILOGUE

Keaton could hear his heart pounding in his ears. Just like every time he was on the battlefield, the beats synced with the ticking of the second hand of a clock. A calm went over him in the face of the danger that awaited him. He inhaled, the oxygen adding fuel to the bravado that came naturally to him. He was a well-trained soldier, a superbly trained warrior. One of the best specimens of the 75th Ranger Regiment.

Stepping out of his hidey-hole where he'd taken cover after the first shots rang out, Keaton looked around. His sightline was clear, which did not bode well. His spidey senses tingled at the calm and quiet. War was a noisy, frenetic affair.

Something was wrong.

Keeping low to the ground, he poked his head out to gather more intel. The camouflage of his clothes made it so that he blended with his environment. Even his gun was painted green and brown to mix in with the elements.

And then he heard it. A cry. A shot.

They sounded one after the other. Keaton's ears perked like a dog coming alert. Before storming into action, he deduced what he'd learned.

The cry had come from the left side. The shot had come from behind him. The blast from the gun had gone over his head. The cry from a human throat had come before the shot. There was no resulting thump of a body.

A tingle went up to his spine. His wife launched herself at him, a paintball gun raised and aiming for his heart. Keaton lowered his weapon and took the missive. The impact made him stagger, but not as much as when Brenda flung herself into his arms.

"Surrender," she said against his lips.

"I never stood a chance," he growled against her mouth.

More shouts rang out behind them, but Keaton ignored the ongoing battle. He'd have waved a white flag of triumph if his hands weren't full of the glory that was his wife.

"Man, you're supposed to have my back," yelled Mac.

Keaton lifted his head to find that Mac was in the same predicament as he was. Lana had fired a number of shots right at his heart as well. Now, her gun was lowered, and she was in his arms. There was a grin on Mac's face as his wife tended to his superficial wounds.

Porco and Spinelli were sitting on the sidelines. The Capulano twins had taken them out in the first few minutes of the paintball game. The two flower child, grown women had sniper sharp aim. Keaton had been ducking them before he'd fallen for his wife.

His little sister sat on the sidelines with Grizz. Well, Patty wasn't so little anymore. Her belly was so big that Keaton worried she might burst at any moment. Beside Patty, Ronnie lounged in the cradle of Rusty's arms. Ronnie's swelling belly was just visible in the outline of her top.

"This was supposed to be a fun excursion in the midst of your insane work plan," said Mac.

"Don't knock the plan," said Keaton.

The plan had been to build the best Ranger training camp in the States. They were well on their way to surpassing that goal. Boots on the Ground was the most sought after school for those wanting to join the 75th Regiment.

But the unexpected had happened. The men had been outmaneuvered. They'd come to this land a tight unit. They'd grown into a strong community and were planting deep roots with the women who'd conquered their hearts. But perhaps, that had been the plan all along.

Shanae Johnson was raised by Saturday Morning cartoons and After School Specials. She still doesn't understand why there isn't a life lesson that ties the issues of the day together just before bedtime. While she's still waiting for the meaning of it all, she writes stories to try and figure it all out. Her books are wholesome and sweet, but her are heroes are hot and heroines are full of sass!

And by the way, the E elongates the A. So it's pronounced Shan-aaaaaaaa. Perfect for a hero to call out across the moors, or up to a balcony, or to blare outside her window on a boombox. If you hear him calling her name, please send him her way!

You can sign up for Shanae's Reader Group at http://bit.ly/ShanaeJohnsonReaders

Also By Shanae Johnson

The Rangers of Purple Heart

The Rancher takes his Convenient Bride

The Rancher takes his Best Friend's Sister

The Rancher takes his Runaway Bride

The Rancher takes his Star Crossed Love

The Rancher takes his Love at First Sight

The Rancher takes his Last Chance at Love

The Brides of Purple Heart

On His Bended Knee

Hand Over His Heart

Offering His Arm

His Permanent Scar

Having His Back

In Over His Head

Always On His Mind

Every Step He Takes

In His Good Hands

Light Up His Life

Strength to Stand

The Rebel Royals series

The King and the Kindergarten Teacher

The Prince and the Pie Maker

The Duke and the DJ

The Marquis and the Magician's Assistant

The Princess and the Principal